I0690179

SWEETMEATS

Children aren't born with prejudice:
They get it from adults.

First Edition

Published by The Nazca Plains Corporation
Las Vegas, Nevada
2012

ISBN: 978-1-61098-308-2
Ebook ISBN: 978-1-61098-309-9

Published by

The Nazca Plains Corporation ®
4640 Paradise Rd, Suite 141
Las Vegas NV 89109-8000

PUBLISHER'S NOTE
Sweetmeats is a work of fiction created wholly by *Lew Bull's* imagination. All characters are fictional and any resemblance to any persons living or deceased is purely by accident. No portion of this book reflects any real person or events.

Cover,
Male Photo - Moori
Henna Design - Artplay

Art Director,
Blake Stephens

*Dedicated to all those who have been
sexually or racially discriminated against
- Have hope and love in your heart.*

SWEETMEATS

*Children aren't born with prejudice:
They get it from adults.*

First Edition

Lew Bull

CONTENTS

CHAPTER 1

The aromatic smell of cooking filled my nostrils and awoke me. I lay in my small bed crammed alongside the beds of my other brothers in our tiny room and I knew that my mother was busy preparing food in our equally tiny kitchen. Although our existence was cramped, we were a relatively happy family. Under our living conditions, which were limited, we made the best of what life had to offer us, that is, except when my father had indulged in the bottle too much, then life could be harsh and his manner brusque.

Our small, plain wood and iron home consisted of two bedrooms, a lounge, kitchen and a bathroom. Surrounding our house was an equally small garden that seemed to have taken on a life of its own, because I never remember seeing anyone from our family working in the garden, either to maintain it or develop it. However, having said that, I cannot condemn anyone in particular because all the houses around us seemed to be in the same condition as ours, small with neglected gardens. I came to believe that Indians were not gardeners and that they would rather let nature take its course.

I was the eldest in our family of four children. I had two younger brothers, aged ten and five, and a baby sister of three years old. This meant that, with the exception of my baby sister, all three of us boys were obliged to help in the home, either preparing dinner, washing dishes, making beds, or any other menial task that my mother allocated to us. I never took offence to having to complete these menial tasks, because I felt it was part of my upbringing, and if it meant helping my mother, whom I dearly loved, then I was happy to help.

I remember one day hearing my mother speaking to our neighbour about us moving from where we lived and this sparked a sense of excitement in my mind. We were about to embark on a mighty journey, but to where, I did not know.

"Where are we going, Amah?" I enquired from my mother when she returned from her conversation with the neighbour.

She smiled at my curiosity and told me that we were moving to a larger house up the road. Initially, my heart sank as I had envisaged a long journey to another world. However, as this was to be a short journey to a larger house, it would allow me to have a room to myself. It also meant that my two brothers would have more space in their room. Naturally I then became excited. It made me feel that I was now a grown-up; I was fourteen at the time.

The day of the move arrived and we excitedly packed and watched as everything went onto the truck, which my father had borrowed from a friend of his, and we moved up the dusty street; we were going up in the world!

Our new house was like a palace. Unlike our previous house, it was made of bricks and had a tiled roof. This was like heaven as we knew that when it rained, we wouldn't be kept awake by the clatter of rain on the tin roof like we had in our old house. In this new brick house we had three bedrooms, a bathroom, lounge, dining room and a kitchen. We also had a large concrete veranda, the floor of which had been polished red, in the front of the house and a fair-sized garden with a few flowering plants and a number of rather elegant looking weeds. At the back of the house there was a garage that had a small room, toilet and shower attached to it, and a wash line. Although we never had a maid working for us, it became apparent to me that this outside accommodation would have been allocated to our maid should we have had one. Instead, my father chose to store his excess 'junk' as my mother called it, in the outside room.

With our move came some new neighbours; but more importantly to me, my very own bedroom. No more would I have to endure the crying of my baby brothers or their constant questioning. At the age of fourteen, it felt as though I had reached adulthood.

As I grew older I felt I was becoming more aware of things not only around me, but about myself as well. I always found it ironic that the suburb in which we lived, called Phoenix, which was on the outskirts of the seaside town of Durban, didn't live up to its name; that is to say, the phoenix being the legendary bird said to set fire to itself and rise anew from the ashes, but the people who lived in this suburb never seemed to rise from anything, except from their beds in the morning.

Within the individual families there was an ethos of pride, but it never revealed itself within the greater community or out on the streets and in the gardens; it stayed firmly entrenched inside the family homes.

With an increase in age, I was occasionally allowed to attend some parties; something that I really looked forward to doing, as there was very little else one could do in Phoenix.

After one such evening of partying and having fun at a friend's house, I awoke early in the morning, even before the birds had started to chirrup. I opened my eyes and looked at the young boy lying on the bed next to me; I looked at his naked white skin and then looked at my own young, brown, Indian body and wondered what attraction he saw in me. Why was he lying there next to me? Why did I invite him to spend the night with me? Was it because we were both slightly drunk, illegally, and wasn't aware of what we were doing? Or was it to challenge the wrongs of our society by sleeping with someone of another colour? I say wrongs, only because we, the Indians in South Africa, didn't have a vote in the government of the day, not that I could have voted, and therefore I challenged their ideological beliefs. I looked at his young, lithe, white body, his chest rising and falling gently as he breathed. I admired his pale, shiny, smooth skin and the thin line of fair hair that traversed from his belly button to his pubic hairs that lay hidden under the sheet that only just covered his genitals. He looked so peaceful lying next to me, but that peace would soon have to be shattered.

The early signs of morning were beginning to reveal themselves. Birds were now beginning to twitter in the trees and the sky was slowly lighting up. I ran a hand gently over his smooth chest. He reacted by turning onto his side to face me and placed an arm over my body. We lay there in each other's arms, pressing our warm bodies together, with me watching his peaceful face. His eyes opened slowly and a smile appeared followed by a gentle, soft kiss.

"It's early; time to get up," I whispered.

"I know, but do we have to?" he enquired, pleadingly.

"We mustn't get caught," I replied, pulling him closer to me in a way suggesting that I didn't want to let him go.

"Will I see you again?" he asked with sadness in his eyes as he searched my face for an answer.

"Definitely, but we have to be careful. It'll be easier for you to get in touch with me, so let's do that. You get a message to me when it's safe and then we can meet again. Of course, you're welcome to come by here anytime during the day, but I must warn you that if you do, there will be some people who will question why a White boy is in an Indian residential area looking for a young Indian boy, and start asking questions. It's much safer to come around in the dark of night when most people are indoors and don't see who is lurking outside in the dark."

"Do your parents know that I stayed here last night?"

"No!" I replied aghast. "That is why we must be careful and why you must leave before they rise."

Both Peter and I pulled on our clothes and I watched as his lithe, well-formed body became clothed, then quietly we emerged from the house, but not before giving each other a kiss on the cheek. I looked around to see that no one was watching and then told Peter that it was all clear for him to 'escape'. Swiftly, and silently, like the prowess of a tiger or lion, he disappeared into the foliage that had grown around the outer fence of our property, and out of sight. I heard his motorbike start up down the road and head away, then I re-entered our house, closed the door behind me and quietly padded back to my room, trying not to disturb the rest of the family, who were still asleep.

"How was your party last night," enquired my mother at the breakfast table.

"It was great thanks, Amah."

"I didn't hear you come in. What time was it?" she asked, pouring a mug of tea for me.

"Oh I don't know, but I know it was after midnight," I replied, digging into my breakfast of porridge.

"Meet any interesting people there?"

With my Mother, whenever we children did anything or went anywhere, we were always given the third degree afterwards. It often felt like we were prisoners being interrogated with all the Who? What? When? Where? Why? -type of questions that were thrown at us. Although I fielded most of them like a well-trained batsman in a cricket match, some needed to be handled with care. Was this line of questioning because of interest or was it merely curiosity to find out about my new developing lifestyle?

"Yes there were some interesting people, but there were so many there that I wasn't able to speak to everyone."

"Oh, who was there?"

My brain kicked into action. Give only the names of those that my Mother knew and whom she liked, and don't mention anything about people of other colours. God forbid that that sort of thing be mentioned because then she'll worry that I might get arrested for contravening the Immorality Act or some other Act promulgated by the all-knowing government of the time; only 'correct' sounding Indian names are mentioned. Having said this, I must point out that although I know that my parents were never given the right to vote in elections by the government of the day, we were all part of the mixed society that made up South Africa in the Apartheid era and were all liable to prosecution if we infringed on any boundary of an Act. Come to think of it, living in South Africa was like an Act! Nothing seemed as it should be.

The party was the first time that I had met Peter and I found him interesting to speak to. He wasn't like other young boys who bragged only about their escapades and conquests; no, he had a brain that delved into books and current issues, which interested me. Yes, he was good-looking, but that wasn't the criteria which had made me decide to invite him back to my home; instead it was his mind that interested me and that's why I wanted to continue this new-found friendship. If the State found out that a White was interacting with a non-White, I certainly could find myself being questioned, not only by my mother, but by people higher up the bureaucratic ladder, and no doubt he would too, the only difference being that I probably would land up in jail, but not him, because of the colour of his skin. To exacerbate the matter even further, heaven forbid that the State should find out that the two people interacting with each other were of the same sex; reverberations would be felt throughout the country.

Peter and I were of different ages; he was seventeen and I was now sixteen, and we went to different schools. He went to a reputable school for White boys, while I went to a co-ed school for Indians. Although our schools were different, I felt sure that both of us received a valuable type of education, although I was later made aware that the Black children of Peter's and my age did not receive a similar education to ours.

In our street, I had now many acquaintances, but friends, very few. Three houses away from ours lived the Chetty's who had, among their five children, a daughter my age by the name of Sarisha, and she and I spent much time together, sharing secrets with each other, especially as we both went to the same school. Sarisha was a very pretty girl and was the only person in whom I confided that I found boys attractive, and often shared my fantasies with her. We were in the same class at school, but I always thought that she was a much brighter learner than me, not that it really bothered me. Occasionally we attended the same parties, but in most cases, Sarisha's parents wouldn't allow her out at night, so it meant that I would have to regale her with the stories of what happened at the parties I attended, much like I would have to do for my mother, the only difference being that Sarisha would always get all the details while my mother received an edited version of the evening's events. Now you might wonder why an Indian boy of sixteen was attending parties. It was just that there was nothing else to do in Phoenix and we couldn't always get into Durban at night, where more entertainment could be found. If we didn't attend parties, we merely stayed at home, reading, talking or listening to the radio, and that in itself could become boring.

Although I have not mentioned my father in detail as yet, it doesn't mean I didn't have one. I definitely had a father, but he was a vociferous, often drunken man who took little interest in our upbringing and left all that to my mother, who was the stoic head of our family, in my eyes. I often thought my father's role in life was merely to procreate and once he had done that, he'd leave everything else to my mother. I also wondered if this was a feature of Indian men in general, and would I turn out that way?

My father spent most of his evenings looking down the neck of a bottle of alcohol, usually Cane Spirits, and taking little interest in his family. Maybe that was the reason my mother asked so many questions of us children because my father showed no interest, but I still loved him, even though he sometimes was abusive to me and my brothers when he was drunk.

I was very fortunate to have my own room in our new home, a rarity in most Indian family's homes as the children often had to share a room together, which would have made Peter's visit difficult. My two brothers shared a room, while my baby sister slept in my parent's room, so this meant that I could, on occasion, bring a friend home.

———————

I couldn't wait to get to school on the Monday to tell Sarisha about Peter.

At first her face was a picture of horror when I told her Peter was a young White boy.

"What if you get caught mixing with Whites?" she enquired with a tone of anxiety in her voice.

"It doesn't worry me," I replied confidently.

"But if they find out that you slept with a White boy?"

"We've only been together once," I replied, gleefully, reminiscing our evening together and ignoring her concern. "And who are they?" I enquired, nonchalantly.

"You know very well," retorted Sarisha. "The police."

"Well as long as you don't say anything, I don't think I have much to worry about."

"And you say you like him, only after one visit?"

I beamed at the thought and nodded in the affirmative.

"Does your mother know?" asked Sarisha, in a sotto voce tone.

"Shh. No," I replied, looking around to see that no one else had heard her question.

"Tell me all about him," said a giggling Sarisha, leading me away from any prying ears. "And when am I going to meet him?"

I began to tell her of my evening out and how I had met Peter and how we had chatted all night and then sneaked back into our house; spent the night together and how he had crept out as the sun rose in the morning, pushing his motorbike down the road for some way before starting the noisy engine. All the while, Sarisha sat transfixed by my story. When I had finished, she squeezed my hand and said, "Is it love, Rajesh?"

I burst out laughing at her comment.

"What is love, little sister? I have only known him for one night. It is too early to tell, but yes, I like him, if that is what you mean."

"Have you got his telephone number?" asked Sarisha.

"Yes, but I must keep it safe so that no-one finds it."

"Are you going to call him again, Raj?"

I beamed at the thought and nodded.

"Maybe on Friday to see if he's free over the weekend," I replied, almost in a dream-like state.

That whole week at school, my mind was wandering all over the place, in fact, it wandered everywhere except towards my schoolwork. Peter was constantly on my mind and every day I would meet Sarisha and we would talk about Peter. Maybe I was in love!

Come Friday midday, I found a public phone, dialled Peter's number and waited for him to pick up the receiver. A sense of excitement ran through my very being as I waited for the phone to be answered. Suddenly a woman's voice was on the other end of the line. Immediately I slammed down the phone. Panic struck me. If I had spoken to her, perhaps she would have been suspicious and asked why an Indian man wanted to speak to her son. I looked at my watch and thought, 'you idiot, Peter will still be at school or on his way home. It's still too early.'

I became a little despondent and Sarisha could see it in my face.

"What's the problem?" she enquired.

"I think it was his mother that answered," I replied.

"So?"

"So, I can't speak to her without her becoming inquisitive of my phone call."

"Oh you are worse than a little girl who is in love. Let me call for you," she continued.

I handed Sarisha the coins for the phone box and watched with baited breath while she dialled the number. I leaned in close to her so that I could hear the ring tone as she held the phone to her ear.

"Hello, 6785247," came the female voice at the other end of the line.

The coins clattered into the box.

"May I speak to Peter, please," said Sarisha, confidently.

"Who may I say is calling?" enquired the female voice.

"Sarisha!"

There was silence on the other end of the line for a while, and then a young male voice was heard.

"Hello!"

"Is that Peter?" enquired Sarisha.

"Yes, who's that?"

"Hello. My name is Sarisha and I'm a friend of Rajesh who wants to speak to you. Just hold on, please."

She handed the receiver to me, beaming.

"He sounds nice," she whispered, and I stood grinning at her before answering.

"Hello, Peter," I said almost whispering, in case his mother could hear my voice.

"Hey, Raj, nice to hear your voice," he replied softly. "How are you?"

"Fine thanks, Peter, and you?"

"I'm ok, but I've been busy this week."

"You're home early, but listen Peter, is your mother standing near the phone?"

"No, why?"

"If she asks about the phone call, just say that Sarisha is a friend from another school that's organising a debating competition between the two schools, and then she may not be suspicious."

"No problem," answered Peter with a chuckle. "But tell me am I going to see you this weekend?"

My heart gave a little flutter when I heard that. Peter actually wanted to see me.

"How about us meeting at the beach tomorrow?" I answered.

"Sure, that sounds like a good idea, but where?"

"Can you get to the Snake Park area then we can walk along the beach away from the 'Whites only' area; away from prying eyes? It should be safe for us to lie in the sand dunes nearer the 'Non-Whites' beach, if that's ok with you."

"That sounds terrific. What time will suit you?" asked Peter.

"Say about eleven o'clock then we can spend the rest of the day there."

"I'll see you there then. Cheers for now."

Peter's phone was put down and I stood there holding my receiver with a grin from ear to ear across my face while Sarisha looked expectantly at me.

"So tell me, what's happening?" she asked excitedly.

I replaced the receiver and said in a low but controlled voice, "We're meeting at the beach tomorrow morning."

She immediately hugged me and we both giggled like typical school girls. I felt I was in heaven having spoken to Peter and knowing that I would see him over the weekend. I sailed away from the public phone booth, with Sarisha close behind, as though I was on some kind of drug or flying in the air.

That evening I told my mother that I was going into the city the next day and would be home in time for dinner, but I never mentioned anything about the beach. I knew that should I say anything about the beach, she might begin to interrogate me and I wouldn't know how to answer her incessant questioning. When I went into my room that night to go to bed, I packed a small backpack with a beach towel and bathing shorts and laid it on the floor next to my bed and went to sleep.

CHAPTER 2

The sun rose bright and early on Saturday morning, and with it, so did I. I pulled on a pair of shorts, a T-shirt and my sandals, put some money in my pocket and went into the kitchen for some breakfast. My two brothers were already there eating their breakfast when I entered the kitchen and they immediately questioned me to find out what I was doing today. When I told then I was going into the city, they also wanted to join me, but I told them that they might get lost in the big city and that it was safer for them to stay at home with Amah. They questioned me to find out why I was going into the city and what I was going to buy for them. I told them I didn't have money to buy presents for them and that I was just going to walk around the city. Naturally, they were very despondent, but I wasn't about to take them to my rendezvous nor did I desire to take responsibility for them.

My mother gave me some sandwiches to take for lunch so I wouldn't have to spend my money unnecessarily and for this I was grateful. I placed the pack of freshly made sandwiches in my backpack, finished my breakfast and went out to catch a non-White's bus to the city.

It must be remembered that this was during the Apartheid era and Whites had their own buses, while we non-Whites had ours. On very rare occasions, and in rural areas, one might find a bus carrying mixed racial groups, but then the non-Whites would have to sit at the rear of the bus.

Throughout the journey into the city, I sat staring out of the window with a supercilious grin on my face, thinking about Peter.

"You seem very happy," said the little, white-haired, old Indian lady sitting beside me in the bus. "Ever since I got on the bus, you have been smiling and smiling," she said.

I merely smiled a little broader at her, but chose not to say anything. Twice she tried to engage me in conversation, but I simply chose to pretend to be deaf and not hear her, which probably irritated her, but I was not about to divulge the secret of my happiness to this unknown person.

After a number of stops and starts, we reached the centre of the city where I disembarked and caught another non-White's bus to the beachfront. This one had fewer people on it so I decided to make for the back seats. I sat staring out of the window and at one stage, caught my own reflection in the window and smiled to myself. I arrived at the Snake Park area early and waited near the toilets for Peter. I watched as men of varying ages went to and from the 'Whites-only' toilets and thought how busy they were at such an early hour of the morning. On one or two occasions, I noticed how some of the men, all White, observed me and some even smiled at me, but I dared not enter this forbidden territory.

After about a fifteen-minute wait, I heard the sound of Peter's motorbike arrive. He got off and greeted me heartily, but without showing any public affection. He parked his bike in a safe area and then we proceeded to walk along the sand away from the 'Whites only' beach, one slightly ahead of the other so as not to draw too much attention to ourselves.

When we had walked for what seemed an eternity, we headed away from the water's edge and went in the direction of the sand dunes, which were covered in shrubs and mangrove-type bushes. These bushes afforded us some shade should we need it and the sand dunes afforded us the privacy we so desired away from prying eyes. We climbed to the top of a sand dune, and descended the other side. Now we could not see the sea and the intensity of the heat from the sand hit us. We quickly headed for some shade and threw down our towels. Standing on the coolness of our towels, we both looked around us to see if we were being watched by anyone. When we had decided we were safe, our arms were flung around the other's body and we hugged each other and our lips met.

"It's so good to see you, again," said Peter, breaking our embrace.

"Same here," I gasped.

Our clothes were instantly removed and Peter slipped into his pale blue Speedo while I pulled on the pair of shorts I had in my backpack. I liked looking at Peter in his tight little Speedo, which enhanced all his male features, and I felt proud to be his friend.

We lay down on our towels, which were placed on one of the sand dune slopes and gazed up into the blazing, blue sky.

"I think I'd better put on some suntan lotion," Peter commented, after a while, as he rose to get some from his beach bag that he had brought. He pulled out a tube of lotion and proceeded to squeeze some of the white lotion onto his chest and arms. He then began rubbing it into his skin. I noticed how his skin immediately began to glisten from the moisture covering his smooth skin.

"Can I help you?" I offered.

"Ok, thanks," replied Peter, handing me the tube.

"Lie back and I'll finish the job for you," I said, squeezing some of the cream onto Peter's legs and beginning to massage it into his skin.

As I worked my way up and down his legs, I could see the outline of his manhood shifting. At one stage I gently, and accidentally, brushed my hand across his crotch and felt his hardness. I smiled, knowingly, but said and did nothing else. When I had completed oiling his legs, I handed him the suntan lotion and lay down on my towel. Not a word was spoken. We lay on the sand like two dead people; neither speaking; just letting the sun warm our bodies.

The heat intensified and sweat trickled down our bodies until the intensity of the heat made it necessary to stand up and move to the top of the sand dunes and catch some of the sea breezes that were blowing, but which we were not getting as we were hidden in the sand dunes.

"I could do with a swim," I said, looking out over the calm, azure sea.

"You go and I'll look after our things here, just in case someone comes and steals them," said Peter.

I ran down the sand dune towards the sea as fast as I could as the sand was burning my feet. Once I was in the cool water, I turned and waved to Peter who was still standing on the top of the sand dune. Once I had cooled down a little in the sea, I ran back up the sand dune to our towels.

"Your turn," I said, breathing heavily having run as fast as I could over the stinging, hot sand.

Peter then sped to the water's edge, his lithe body seemingly gliding like a mirage over the heated sand. Once he too had cooled down in the water, he headed back to the towels, throwing his body onto his towel as the sand burnt the soles of his feet.

We lay on our backs, staring up at the clear blue sky, as trickles of water slid down our sides and faces. I felt the touch of Peter's fingers glance over my fingers as we lay next to each other; then I felt his clasp and the squeeze of his hand around mine, but neither of us spoke. I glanced over towards him and saw that he was watching me. I smiled, white teeth glistening in the sunshine; my dark skin contrasting against his fair skin. He smiled back, but still no word was spoken. I could feel an arousal in my shorts and became concerned that someone might come over the top of the sand dune and see us, so I withdrew my hand from his. He had a puzzled look on his face as I did this, but I still smiled. I glanced down at Peter's waist and Speedo and noticed that he was fully aroused, but I was afraid to do anything.

Eventually, Peter stood up, went up to the top of the sand dune, looked down at the sea from the top of the dune, obviously checking to see if anyone was approaching, turned and headed into the mangrove shrubs, disappearing from sight. For a moment I lay there on the towel, and then I too stood up, looked out from the top of the sand dune, and then went into the mangrove shrubs after Peter. He was standing in the cool shade waiting for me. As I approached him, he stretched out his arms and gathered me into them and pulled me close to him. Our bodies rubbed together and we felt each other's urgency. Slowly we sank to the soft, cool, shaded sand and began to make love.

As we emerged from our hideout, the intensity of the heat once again hit us.

"Let's take our stuff and go down to the water for a swim," suggested Peter.

I agreed, but before we left the sanctuary of the sand dunes, Peter once more held me in his arms and our lips met. It made me feel good and secure to be in the arms of someone who seemed to care for me.

We sped over the scorching sand, dropping our bags just before we reached the cool water. Our bodies almost sizzled as we hit the water and felt its refreshing tingle over our hot bodies. We splashed and laughed, innocently, and splashed and touched until we felt ready to emerge from the coolness.

After spending some time, lying near the water's edge, we decided to it was time to return to where we had first met. We slowly walked back to the 'Whites' only' beach along the water's edge so as to avoid the heat of the soft sand. As we neared the spot where Peter's bike was parked, we stopped and looked into each other's eyes.

"Today has been wonderful, Raj," he said.

"For me too," was my only reply. "Will you contact me?"

"Sure I will," replied Peter, "Maybe tomorrow, if that's ok with you?"

I smiled and nodded. I couldn't wait to hear from Peter again, even though we hadn't departed from each other yet.

At the motor bike, Peter offered to take me home on his bike, but I said 'no' because it would mean not only explaining to my family, but any people seeing a Black and White together on a motorbike might become suspicious, so he said he would wait with me at the bus station, to which I agreed.

We stood and chattered for a while at the bus station and then Peter left as soon as my bus arrived. I was sad to see him go, but inside of me there was a happiness that I'd not felt before and which I found difficult to explain, but this had to remain my secret; well, mine and Sarisha's.

On my arrival back home, my two brothers wanted to know what the city was like.

"Busy," I replied, "With lots of people shopping."

"Did you buy anything?" they chorused.

"No," I answered, expecting them to be upset that I had not brought them anything. "Not even any sweets, because I didn't have enough money."

They seemed happy with my answer and ran off to their room, but my mother obviously wanted more details.

"Did you not buy anything, Raj?" enquired my mother.

"No, Amah. I looked at all the beautiful things in the shop windows but they are far too expensive to buy."

I knew that my mother very seldom ventured into the city, so if anyone of our family did go, she would love to hear their stories of what they had seen and what was in the shops to buy.

"Did you meet any of your friends?" continued the conversation.

I knew where this might land me, so I became very cautious as to how I answered her questions.

"I saw one or two, but just to wave to. We didn't speak as they were on the other side of the busy street," I offered as a story.

"Hm, I see. And who were these friends, my darling?"

"Just friends from school, Amah. Where's Apah?" I asked, trying to change the subject and find out where my father was.

As we spoke, and before she could respond, Krishna, the younger of my two brothers ran in carrying my damp shorts that I had used for swimming.

"Rajie," he shouted with glee, "These are wet. Did you wet yourself?"

"Of course not," I replied rather indignantly as I snatched the damp shorts away from him.

"Oh! Why are they wet, Raj?" asked my mother, somewhat perplexed.

"It was so hot in the city that I decided to go for a swim in the sea."

"But where did you swim? Not at the Whites' beach surely?"

"Of course not! I'm not that stupid to do such a thing. I walked to the Indian beach."

"But that is so far," said my mother, looking pained as she said it.

"What's this about going to the beach?" said my father, as he entered the lounge.

I looked at both him and my mother. The former was drunk while the latter was interested in my day's outing.

"The boy and I were just talking about his day out," said my mother, knowing that to say the wrong thing to my father when he was in this condition, was tantamount to looking for disaster.

"Have you been smoking?" leered my father, breathing alcohol fumes into my face as he questioned me.

"No, Apah, why would you ask something like that? I just went into the city to do some shopping," I replied, backing away from the smell.

I could tell that he hadn't been at his usual Cane Spirits, but had been sharing Whiskey with someone else.

"The boy has money to spend," he continued, sarcastically, "but he contributes nothing to this house."

"I don't earn a living, Apah. I'm still at school."

"So where do you steal this money from, hey?"

He grabbed me by the throat and started to squeeze. His eyes, although blood-shot from the alcohol, stared wide-eyed at me like some lunatic's might. I screamed as best I could, more out of fright than anything else. My brothers came running to see what the commotion was about and at the same time, my mother shouted at him, striking out at him as well.

"Leave the boy alone. I gave him the money."

She had lied to cover for me. In fact I never had much money; only enough to pay for my bus fares to and from the city.

My father struck me across the side of my head, sending me reeling and bumping my head on the floor and making my nose bleed. I scrambled away from him as fast as I could before he could aim a kick at me, and all the time my mother and two brothers were screaming and crying aloud. My father continued to hurl verbal abuse at me as I scampered to the front door and fled the house and ran speedily down the road to Sarisha's house. I frantically rapped on the door when I arrived there. Sarisha's mother opened it and saw my bloodied face.

"Dear child, what has happened to you?"

I burst into tears when I entered the safety of her home. She called Sarisha and between the two of them, they began to clean up my bloody face. Naturally I was embarrassed to tell them the truth of what had happened, but then most of the people in our street knew of my father's drinking and behaviour, so it wasn't really necessary to say much more to them.

"You stay here tonight, Raj," said Sarisha's mother. "Have you eaten?"

I told her that I had not, so a place was prepared at their table for me to partake in supper with them.

That night Sarisha and I sat together and I regaled her once more with my heavenly stories of Peter and our day at the beach; of course I didn't tell her about the bit in the mangrove bushes because I didn't think she'd like to hear about that, but my night spent in their house was blissful in the sense that there was no drunkenness or fighting and I peacefully fell asleep thinking of Peter and not of the shame that my father was bringing to me.

CHAPTER 3

A week after the incident with my father, who incidentally never mentioned another word about it, grave news was delivered to us; his father, my grandfather, had passed away, so it meant a journey to Chatsworth, a nearby suburb, to pay our respects to his wife, my Granny. This was my first death and I wasn't sure whether I should treat it as an auspicious occasion or not. My mother had explained to me what was expected of us as his grandchildren, and that we would have to visit my Granny to sympathise with her. I knew that there probably wouldn't be very many people my age there, so I asked if I could invite Sarisha to accompany us; to which my mother agreed, provided Sarisha's mother was agreeable.

My father, mother, two brothers, baby sister, Sarisha and I all climbed into our old Datsun motorcar, squashing each other in the process. To us children, there was an element of excitement because we were going on a trip, but to my mother and father, it was a sombre occasion, and often along the journey, we children were regularly chided for laughing and giggling too loudly. Naturally my younger brothers never understood the occasion, other than we were going to visit Granny.

We eventually arrived at Granny's house where we could hear much wailing and keening coming from the inside of the crowded house.

"Now children, you are to remain outside while your father and I go in to see your Granny, do you understand?"

We all looked rather bewildered by this statement, as we usually rushed into Granny's house, shouting and screaming, but we agreed to do as we were told. Through the front window, which looked into Granny's lounge, I could see my Aunty Ashra and Aunty Selvie sitting there in deep conversation with each other, while a number of strange women were wailing at the top of their voices, with Granny sitting next to the laid out body of my grandfather. This was indeed a strange sight for me.

Both aunties were my father's younger sisters and both were attractive to the eye but neither had children my age, so I seldom visited them unless it was a family occasion when everyone was expected to attend.

Granny's lounge was a clutter of heavy Imbuia furniture mainly of the ball and claw kind. There was a three-seater couch, two solid easy chairs, all with highly decorated padded cushions, and a low coffee table on which stood an arrangement of plastic carnations; it all seemed very funereal. Those who could find a seat sat on one; otherwise people were obliged to sit on the carpeted floor. Around the walls and on some of the furniture were photographs of every member of Granny's family. Some of these photos were so old that they were not only faded, but resembled some faded past which I never knew.

I looked through the window at the old man lying there, his hands across his chest and he looked ever so peaceful that I thought he was just asleep. Obviously it was going to be a long sleep. Outside of the front door stood Uncle Harry and Uncle Sivan, my aunties' husbands, smoking. My father, immediately after having greeted Granny, went out to the two men and began chatting to them, while my mother remained indoors.

"Look who's come to see you," wailed my Granny on seeing my mother, but talking to my 'sleeping' grandfather. "Vanitha has come all the way from Phoenix to see you, isn't that wonderful of her to do that, Dada," she continued, as though my grandfather was wide awake and paying attention to what she was saying.

My mother had not gone empty-handed to Granny's house and had brought food with her, so on seeing the pots that my mother was carrying, Granny lifted the lid of one, sniffed the air and smelt the curry and then returned to talking to my sleeping grandfather.

"Look at the nice pot of curry Vanitha has brought; it's your favourite and you're not going to be able to eat any. Ooh Dada," wailed my Granny.

"Why did you go and die like this? Why wasn't it me? Ooh Dada, take me with you."

Her wailing increased in velocity as she rocked too and fro, while grandfather remained motionless.

By this time, my two brothers, Niven and Krishna, had joined Sarisha and me at the window, so four small faces peered in, watching this tableau.

"Raj, why is grand daddy sleeping in the lounge and not in his bedroom?" enquired Krishna, my baby brother.

I looked at Sarisha for guidance, but none was forthcoming as she was too interested in the wailing going on in the lounge.

"Raj, I asked you…"

"Yes, I heard what you asked."

"So, why is he sleeping in the lounge and in the day time too?"

I looked down at my little brother who was standing on tiptoe to peer through the window.

"He's just very tired and decided it was easier to sleep there than go all the way to his bedroom," I answered.

Sarisha spun a look of dismay at me, but before she could open her mouth to say anything, I glared at her as if to say 'don't say a word'.

"Then why is Granny crying?" continued Krishna.

"Because she doesn't like him sleeping there," was all I could think of saying.

"Then why doesn't she wake him up and tell him to go to bed, like mummy says to us some times?"

"Sh!" I said trying to stop him from asking any more questions.

A moment of silence fell among us children, but the wailing and keening never let up in the lounge. Granny kept rocking back and forth as she fired questions at my sleeping grandfather. I watched and listened; then I realised what my English teacher had taught us in class: these were all rhetorical questions because my grandfather was not answering her back. Suddenly English became meaningful for me.

While we stood outside watching the goings on in the lounge, more people from my Granny's street started to arrive to pay their respects. Soon the lounge was filled with wailing women, each one trying to wail louder than the person next to her. Eventually, both Sarisha and I saw the funny side to this scenario and we burst out laughing. Aunty Selvie, who was my favourite Aunty, heard us and threw us a dirty look. I immediately knew that

I had done wrong. Eventually, my mother came out and said that we must come inside and greet Granny.

"Greet Granny, and don't ask questions," said my mother, glaring at us children.

When Granny saw us, her crying became almost hysterical and her rocking became so exaggerated that at one stage I thought she would fall over where she sat.

"Oh look, Dada," she wailed, "The children have come to see you. Oh why did it have to be you? Take me with you, Dada. It should have been me and not you. Look how nice the children have dressed to come and see you and all you do is sleep!"

We stood watching her and staring at my sleeping grandfather, not knowing what we were expected to do or say. Then Krishna broke the ice.

"Can I wake him up?" asked Krishna, venturing a little closer to have a look.

"No!" I hissed and caught his arm before he could go prodding grandfather's sleeping body.

"Raj, you and Sarisha take your brothers to the kitchen and help there if they need any assistance," said my mother, glaring at us as she desperately tried to get us out of the way before we said or did something untoward.

We entered the kitchen, and through the back door we saw the men now gathered in the back yard, passing a bottle of clear liquid, which wasn't water, to one another and each pouring a little from it into a glass. I knew what this was and wondered how long it would take before my father became inebriated and started embarrassing himself and his family.

One of the women asked us if we were hungry, to which both Niven and Krishna replied that they were, so plates of delicious looking curry were dished up for the four of us. We took our plates and ventured out into the back yard to eat. Niven and Krishna sat together on the top step outside of the back door, while Sarisha and I ventured towards an avocado pear tree for some shade.

The men, by this time, were beginning to become a little louder in their conversations, probably as a result of the clear liquid, and soon jokes were being cracked and laughter was filtering into the house. Soon one of the women from the kitchen emerged and scolded them for disrespecting my Granny, so they quietened down a little, but not for long.

Before we had finished eating, my mother emerged from the kitchen to check on us children. She saw my father and spoke quietly into his ear, probably telling him not to disgrace himself or us, and then she returned to the kitchen to get some food for herself. Soon others were following suit and some of the visitors came out to the avocado pear tree to join us children. Even Granny broke her wailing to fill her stomach with food and it was during this time that Krishna disappeared, having finished his helping of food.

No one really noticed Krishna's absence and it wasn't until he re-emerged from the kitchen in tears that we were aware that there was a problem.

"What is it my child?" enquired my mother, taking Krishna in her arms and hugging him tenderly.

"It's grand daddy," wailed the child, tears streaming down his brown cheeks.

"What about him?" asked my mother.

"He's not waking up," continued Krishna.

My mother looked a little perplexed especially as she had not explained the concept of death to my little brothers. Perhaps now was the time to explain death and its consequences to little Krishna.

"How do you know he's not waking up, Krishna, darling?" asked my mother, hoping for an easy way to explain my grandfather's demise.

"I went into the lounge and shook him…"

"You shook him!" exclaimed my mother, rising and rushing indoors to the lounge.

Granddaddy was still lying where they had left him, but his shroud looked a little dishevelled. My mother looked down at his wizened face and tidied the shroud.

"Why doesn't he move when I push him?" asked Krishna.

"Come my child, let me talk to you and tell you why," said my mother, taking Krishna up into her arms and carrying him out into the front garden.

They were gone for some time, and when they returned to the back yard where the others were, Krishna looked ashen but calm, so I assumed that my mother had explained life and death to him, but whether he understood these concepts was debatable.

After everyone had eaten, the adults traipsed back into the lounge where Granddaddy was still lying. The women resumed their wailing while the men resumed their consumption of the clear liquid in the backyard. By now my father was well on his way to becoming inebriated. I watched how he almost swooned on Uncle Harry, who was a rather stout, yet sturdy man with a well-shaped black moustache that tickled when he kissed us children. Uncle Harry supported my father and prevented him from falling over. When he saw that we were watching their behaviour, he joked with my father and said "this wind is blowing so strong it's almost toppling us over." I knew otherwise, but Niven and Krishna giggled as they watched the two men supporting each other.

By five in the afternoon, we left Granny's house and returned home, but this time the children travelled with Aunty Selvie, because Uncle Harry was driving our Datsun as my father was unable to find even the gears, let alone steer the car in a straight line.

When we arrived home, Sarisha returned to her home while we made our way into our house.

"Bath time, little ones," shouted my mother as we entered the house and Uncle Harry helped my father into our lounge.

"One for the road, Harry?" slurred my father as Uncle Harry placed him in an easy chair in our lounge.

"I don't think so," admonished Aunty Selvie.

She was a tall, elegant woman whom I thought didn't match Uncle Harry. I would have thought that Aunty Selvie would have married a slim, good-looking young man, rather than a fat ordinary man; but then maybe Uncle Harry had more money than the slim, good-looking men! Be that as it may, I liked her because I thought she was modern in her thinking and probably more broad-minded than anyone else in our direct family.

She and I sat down in the lounge while my mother and Uncle Harry persuaded my father to have a lie down on his bed, in the hopes that he might sober up or sleep right through until the next morning.

"How are you doing at school, Raj?" asked Aunty Selvie.

"Fine, Aunty," I replied, knowing how important it was to do well at school, and how much emphasis our families placed on education.

"And have you found yourself a little girlfriend yet?" she continued, smiling angelically at me.

I know I blushed, but it didn't really show through the colour of my skin. How could I tell her the truth?

"Sarisha and I are good friends," I responded, hoping that she would accept that Sarisha was my girlfriend. Heaven help the nation had I told her that I had a boyfriend; but who was I to assume that Peter was my boyfriend, after all, we weren't in some permanent relationship; the government wouldn't allow such behaviour – two boys together and a White and an Indian boy to add insult to injury!

She smiled once more at me, but this time there seemed to be a different look in her eyes, almost a knowing look, a look of understanding and acceptance.

We continued our conversation, talking about books and music, theatre and films, but my knowledge of most of these subjects was unfortunately limited. I wished that I could go to the theatre, but we were limited to going only to Indian performances. Yes, we also had Indian cinemas, but they showed mostly Tamil or Hindi language films, and my knowledge of those languages was extremely limited, so I seldom, if ever, ventured into the cinemas.

There was a place in Grey Street, in Durban, which we all called the 'Bug House' which showed more commercial films in English, continuously throughout the day and evening, and I had on occasion slipped into its dark realms to sit in the back row and watch cowboy and comedy films, but I never told my parents of these ventures, so I wasn't about to divulge this information to Aunty Selvie who might tell my mother. However, this conversation with Aunty Selvie, did trigger off a thought that perhaps I might be able to invite Peter to the 'Bug House' and we could sneak in and watch a film together, hopefully without the interference of the police or some other bureaucratic official; and so I decided to put my plan into action.

CHAPTER 4

Before my plans for the 'Bug House' could materialise, great excitement occurred in our house; my mother informed me one day that Aunty Selvie had contacted her asking whether she and Uncle Harry could take me to see a live theatre show. This was the most exciting news that I had ever heard. I had never had occasion to attend a live show, let alone enter a theatre, unlike the 'bug house'. I begged my mother to please let me go with them, because there were going to be singers and dancers, acts and comedians; something I had read about, but never experienced in my short life.

Aunty Selvie and Uncle Harry lived in what can only be described as a baronial mansion in Reservoir Hills near the University of Durban-Westville where both my aunties had studied, and they had suggested to my mother that I go with them to the theatre, which was situated on the University campus, and stay the night at their home after the show. After much pleading, my mother relinquished and said that I could attend the concert but I was obviously to be on my best behaviour, which I promised.

On the Saturday of the concert, I packed a small suitcase with clothes and my father drove me to Reservoir Hills in our rather dilapidated Datsun motor car, to Aunty Selvie's house.

It was a sprawling four-bedroom home set on a hill overlooking everything around it, and from its spacious veranda, one could sit comfortably in their outdoor furniture and see the blue of the sea in one direction, and the green of the countless sugar cane fields in the other direction. Against these backdrops stood numerous large properties, all belonging to wealthy Indian families. Reservoir Hills can only be described as the elite area among the Indian community, and although we were all living in a country whose laws excluded some racial groups from others, within the Indian community, there was an element of self chosen segregation; a 'them and us' scenario. However, as I was to learn as I was growing up, that this phenomenon existed in many societies, not just among the Indian communities.

On our arrival, Aunty Selvie showed me to my room while Uncle Harry and my father sat on the veranda, enjoying a smoke together. My room was nothing like the one I had in our house; it was large, airy and beautifully furnished. However, that is not to say that my parents never furnished our house to the best of their budget. I couldn't resist bouncing on the bed that had been offered to me, to see how much softer it was than the one I had at home.

It was mid-afternoon when I arrived and after placing my small suitcase in my room, Aunty Selvie and I went out onto the veranda to join the men.

"Are you excited about the concert tonight?" enquired Aunty Selvie, pouring me a glass of lemonade.

"Very!" I exclaimed, beaming broadly. "Do you and Uncle go to the theatre much?" I asked, sipping from my glass.

"Oh, as often as we can. There are always shows being performed here at the university and I enjoy going to them."

"Your aunty studied drama, you see, Raj," interjected Uncle Harry, beaming proudly at his wife.

"That's wonderful. Where?" I asked enthusiastically.

"Here at Durban-Westville," she replied.

"Is that why you speak so beautifully?" I enquired.

"I suppose you could say so. We had a wonderful professor who always spoke beautifully and I suppose we copied him. When he opened his mouth you just sat in awe and listened to his mellow, well-articulated voice floating through the air of the lecture theatre to reach your ears. Professor Smith was a wonderful man," she said, almost dream-like.

"Smith," I repeated. "That is not an Indian name."

"Oh no," replied Aunty Selvie. "He was White."

"But I thought that Whites and us couldn't mix because of the government's rules," I innocently asked.

"In theory, yes. Apartheid means that we are supposed to be separate and that Blacks and Whites can't mix, but nearly all our lecturers were White. I would call them radicals who fought to see that we had a proper education."

"But wouldn't they get into trouble for mixing with the Indians?" I continued.

"Not if the sun was shining," replied Aunty, smiling as she said it.

"I don't understand."

"Think about it. Do you see Whites walking down Grey Street in the heart of Durban, during the day, along with the Indian and Black people?"

I thought for a moment and then replied that I had.

"Well, that is what I mean by when the sun shines. It seems that it's acceptable for us to mix when it comes to business practices, but once the sun sets and the police can't see in the dark, then we have to go our own separate ways. You see it's all linked to economics. It's the same with the Japanese and the Chinese."

"What do you mean by Chinese and Japanese Aunty Selvie?"

"Because the South African government trades with Japan, the Japanese are regarded as honorary Whites, but because they don't trade with China, the Chinese living here are regarded the same as us: non-Whites."

This whole Apartheid thing became a little confusing to me; it existed in the dark but not in the day!

"So, for example," I continued, hesitantly, "it's fine for me to walk and talk to a White friend during the day, but I mustn't be caught or seen doing it in the night?"

"That's a very simplistic way of putting it," answered Aunty Selvie, "but I suppose if you want to understand it like that, then yes. The bottom line is that you mustn't sleep with anyone of another colour, according to the government," she said, almost whispering these last words. "The government created what they called the Immorality Act!"

I must have had a startled look on my face when she uttered these last words, because she noticed and said to me, "Is something wrong, Raj?"

I stammered for a moment and then said, "What's this Immorality Act that you mentioned?"

"It was an Act brought in by the government which made it criminal for two people of different racial groups to fall in love with each other."

This puzzled me more and Aunty Selvie could see that.

"What I mean, Raj, is that you couldn't have sex together if you were from different racial groups."

"It still doesn't make sense to me, Aunty Selvie."

"No, my darling, Apartheid, segregation, whatever you want to call it, doesn't make sense," she smiled, "after all, we're all human beings together."

I sat sipping my lemonade, but in deep thought. Did this mean that the night Peter and I had spent together could land me in very serious trouble because he was White and I was Indian? I remained silent for some time, but noticing that every now and again Aunty Selvie passed a glance in my direction. I didn't want to get into trouble and neither did I want Peter to get into trouble for something that both of us found as being innocent.

Soon my father said that he should be making his way back home, so we bid him goodbye and he drove off in his Datsun back to Phoenix and I was left alone with Aunty Selvie.

"You have been very quiet most of this afternoon," she commented. "Is something the matter; something troubling you?"

"No," I spluttered.

"Is there something bothering you that you want to talk about?" she continued.

Again I spluttered that there wasn't anything troubling me. I couldn't tell Aunty Selvie about Peter and me and our night together. Instead she decided to leave questioning me while she went off to see that the dinner was being prepared. I sat contemplating what had been said and trying to understand the 'day / night' issues of Apartheid and the Immorality Act, while Uncle Harry sat quietly smoking.

After a delicious dinner, I bathed and changed for the evening's show. Aunty Selvie looked most glamorous in a beautiful sari of varying shades of red and gold. Her gold jewellery, which I knew was important to any well-bred Indian woman, glittered in the light and she looked just like a queen. Even Uncle Harry looked smart.

As we drove along Pitlochry Road and into Varsity Road to enter the university grounds, I kept thinking about this Apartheid thing and my relationship with Peter, but once we arrived at the parking area and emerged from the car, all thoughts of Apartheid were diminished, especially when I saw the crowds of people arriving.

Cars were arriving by the hundreds and the most glamorous and beautiful people were emerging from them. I can understand why Aunty Selvie looked like she did; this was like a fashion show and each woman seemed to be trying to outdoor the next. There was so much gold jewellery that one was almost blinded by wealth. I soon realised that even in our Indian society there must be a form of Apartheid because I had never seen such wealth. I even began to wonder whether, just as we sometimes called the Whites 'larnies', perhaps we had 'larnies' among the Indian community.

We made our way into the plush theatre and took our seats. The regal red colour of the velvet seats matched that of the scarlet curtains that divided the stage area from us in the auditorium. I had never seen such lavishness. There was quite a hubbub of noise and everyone chattered excitedly. Greetings were made and people waved to friends that they caught sight of and a sense of excitement pervaded the theatre. Soon the theatre lights were dimmed and the show began. The sense of excitement even struck me and I shifted so that I was sitting upright in my seat, in anticipation of what was to come.

The plush stage curtains opened and there in the centre of the stage was a middle-aged man sitting alone, cross-legged, playing a sitar. I listened to the music emanating from this instrument and became entranced by its melodious sound; then while he was playing, two young girls emerged from the side of the stage and began to do a dance. The sight and the sound was so hypnotic, I was drawn to the edge of my seat and leant forward to absorb this magical moment. I caught Aunty Selvie's eye and she smiled at me. When it finished, everyone applauded wildly, myself included.

A man and a woman singing soon followed this act: but I didn't think much of their song. I suppose I had been spoilt listening to the radio and the music on it, because this I found shrill and unpleasant to the ear, but the rest of the audience seemed to enjoy it.

Suddenly a loud drumming was heard and onto the stage ran twenty young men and women who performed a very energetic dance that once again entranced me. Although I sat focussing on the dance and was caught up in the beat of the music, I couldn't prevent myself from admiring some of the young men. They looked lithe and strong and had smooth, clean faces, and their bodies gyrated sexily to the music. A smile broke on my face as I watched the athleticism of these young dancers: maybe one day I might be able to dance like that, I thought.

The show continued for another hour or so, then the stage curtains closed once more and the theatre lights were switched on and I looked bewildered. Uncle Harry saw my expression and reassured me that the show wasn't over, but that it was interval. This was the time for the men and women to gather in their separate groups to chat and gossip. I wasn't sure whether I should follow Uncle Harry or Aunty Selvie, so I sort of wandered into no-man's-land. I stood in the foyer of this grand theatre and looked around me, admiring both the people and the interior. While I was standing there, I heard a voice behind me call my name so I turned around.

"Hi Raj. What are you doing here?"

As I turned I saw it was it was a boy from my school, but in a standard above mine.

"Oh, hello, Morgan. I'm here with my aunty and uncle," I replied.

Morgan was a boy who was sporty, unlike me, and was captain of the First Cricket team, so I seldom had much to say to him at school, but I had noticed him around the grounds. He was tall and slim with a friendly face, but because of my lack of interest in sport, I had never had occasion to become friendly with him. In fact, I was quite surprised to see him at a cultural event like this concert and that he knew my name.

"What are you doing here?" I enquired. "I thought you preferred sport to cultural events," I said.

"I'm here with my parents. I don't mind the occasional concert, but I'm not really keen on straight theatre; you have to think too much then," he said, laughing. When he laughed, a row of gleaming white teeth emerged and I thought, 'what a lovely smile you possess and what a good looking face you have', but I couldn't tell him that.

We stood and made small talk, while Aunty Selvie mingled with her socialite friends. A buzz of excitement enveloped the crowd in the foyer and I felt myself being caught up in it. Eventually, a bell started to ring, warning the audience that the second half of the show was about to commence. Morgan and I said our farewells, and I headed back to my seat. When Aunty Selvie and Uncle Harry returned, she asked me to whom I had been talking.

"It's a boy from my school," I answered, without revealing too much information about him.

"Is he in your class at school?" she continued.

"No, he's actually a standard above me and he's more interested in sport than academics."

"That surprises me," said Aunty Selvie. "He looks as though he might be an academic sort of person."

"He's captain of the First Cricket team," I responded, "but I'm not sure that he's too bright," I added, after a thought.

I saw Morgan return to his seat which was about three rows in front of ours and to the left. I noticed how Aunty Selvie watched with interest as he moved along the row and then sat down, and then she turned to me and smiled; why I don't know.

After a moment, she said, "He looks quite a nice young man, Raj."

I wasn't quite sure what she meant by that statement, but I smiled at her and nodded in agreement. Yes, Morgan did look like a nice young man. I also noticed how Morgan kept turning around to see who was sitting around the theatre, and then he caught sight of me and grinned his toothy smile. I smiled back, and so did Aunty Selvie.

The theatre lights began to dim and soon the second half of the show was underway. There was more singing and dancing, more laughter and more beautiful performers, and throughout the second half of the show, I noticed my attention was on both the performers on stage and on the back of Morgan's head. At the end of the show, I applauded enthusiastically, but then so did the rest of the audience. As we made our way out of the theatre, I thanked both Uncle Harry and Aunty Selvie for inviting me to join them at the concert. I also caught Morgan's eye as we left and smiled a goodbye at him.

On the way home, we chatted animatedly about the show and Aunty Selvie was able to tell me some of the more technical things about the show, which I appreciated.

"Why don't you stay for lunch tomorrow?" she suggested to me.

I hesitated, but before I could respond, she added, "Would you like to invite your friend from the show to join us?"

"I don't have his phone number and I don't know where he lives," I replied, with a mixed feeling of sadness and relief; sadness, because it would have been enjoyable to get to know Morgan, but relief because I might have to explain my feelings to Aunty Selvie.

"Pity. I'm sure you would have enjoyed having some company, but never mind, perhaps another time."

We left the subject there and when we got home I decided it was time for me to go to bed, so I said goodnight to Uncle Harry and Aunty Selvie and made my way to my room. My bed was definitely softer than the one I had at home and soon, after I had snuggled under the blankets, I was in dreamland, dreaming of the young men, the beautiful costumes, and interspersed among this, Morgan's smiling face.

The following morning, after breakfast, I asked if I could return home as I had homework to do, so Uncle Harry drove me back. I thanked both of them for the wonderful evening and hoped that they would let me

know if there were more shows appearing at the theatre, then I might ask my
father to take me there.

Once back at home, I rushed down the road to Sarisha's house to tell
her of my evening out.

"You should have seen all the fine clothes the ladies were wearing,"
I gabbled to her excitedly, "and the dancing and the dancers, ooh, they were
all beautiful."

She sat listening with a fixed smile on her face. She wanted to know
all the details about my aunty's sari, the clothes of the other women, what
the men looked like, especially the male dancers and singers and what the
theatre was like.

"What are the other half like?" she joked.

"What do you mean the other half?" I enquired.

"You know, the wealthy, the Reservoir Hills snobs."

Immediately I thought she was referring to Aunty Selvie and Uncle
Harry, so I was somewhat defensive.

"My Aunty Selvie is not a snob!" I exclaimed.

"I don't mean your family," she answered, "I'm talking about those
others, and I'm sure there were many there at the theatre."

I then realised to what she was referring. If I thought of my family
and how and where we lived, I realised that we didn't fit in with the Reservoir
Hills snobs, as Sarisha called them. Sure Uncle Harry had money, but then
he owned three clothing factories and that was how he'd made his money.
Aunty Selvie was an ordinary woman who had trained to be a teacher, but
who had married into money, so I didn't see them as snobs, but then maybe
I didn't fully understand what Sarisha was getting at.

"It's the 'them and us' syndrome," she rambled on. "It's just like the
Apartheid system but within our own kind."

Aunty Selvie had tried to explain some aspects of the Apartheid
system to me, but I had never thought of our own kind carrying out similar
things to each other. I must have looked horrified, because Sarisha tried
to soften the shocked blow by adding, "It happens in all societies, Raj, so
don't feel so bad about it. There's always the wealthy and the poor. Even the
Whites have it. I'm not sure if the Blacks have it, but who knows, perhaps
they do."

I decided to change the subject, so I told her about Morgan being at the theatre.

"Morgan was there?" she asked, sounding shocked. "But he doesn't seem the type that would put a foot in a theatre, unless it was an operating theatre because of some sporting injury that he'd received," she continued. "I can't believe it."

"It's true. He even came over and spoke to me. He actually seems quite a nice person," I ventured to say.

"I want to see if he speaks to you on Monday when we're back at school," taunted Sarisha, shaking her head in disbelief that the young man had spoken to me. "Maybe it's another case of the 'them and us' syndrome within our own school.

"Why shouldn't he speak to me?" I enquired.

"Has he ever spoken to you before?" she replied.

"No," I hesitantly answered.

"Well, there you see. It was probably to impress those around him why he spoke to you, but when his cricket friends are around him at school, he might be embarrassed to speak to you."

"I don't see why he wouldn't speak to me," I replied, trying to understand Sarisha's argument.

"Well, we'll see at school."

I didn't want to argue with Sarisha, because I knew it would be pointless, so I changed the subject back to the show itself and even gave her an attempted version of the dancing that I'd seen in the show, much to her delight and derision, but I must confess that after I had finished telling her of the evening, I still wondered if Morgan would talk to me at school on Monday.

CHAPTER 5

Monday arrived and I set off for school, wondering whether Morgan would even speak to me in front of his other friends. I caught the bus with Sarisha and as we travelled, so the bus filled up with more and more chatting children, all relating to one another what they had done over the weekend. Sarisha and I sat together, huddled up in deep conversation about Morgan. She confessed that she had once looked at him and thought him good-looking, but when she realised that he wasn't that bright, she became arrogant and dismissed him from her thoughts, but now that I had mentioned his name and he had been resurrected, so to speak, in her memory, she was now beginning to have second thoughts about the boy.

The bus crawled along the winding road almost as though it was on its last legs, until it reached our school, where the occupants spewed out into the road. We entered the gates of the school and made our way to our classrooms in order to drop off our suitcases and satchels, and then we went out into the grounds to mingle until the bell rang for the start of school. I looked out for Morgan, but didn't see him.

"Do you see him?" asked Sarisha.

I shook my head. "Maybe we'll see him during break," I suggested.

Just as the school bell rang and we started to head to our various classrooms, I caught sight of him. He looked so ordinary in his school uniform, unlike the sight that I had seen on Saturday evening when he was dressed in smart jeans and a silk shirt, unbuttoned a little way down his chest.

Throughout the morning session of school, my thoughts were on my work, until the bell for break awakened my interest of being able to sit and chat with my friends in the school ground.

I found a bench under one of the trees and sat there waiting for Sarisha and some of her friends to join me. While I sat there, I heard Morgan's voice behind me.

"Hi there, how's it?" he enquired.

I turned and smiled. He was with some of his friends whom I really didn't care for, so my smile diminished somewhat on seeing them.

"Hi," I replied.

I wasn't sure whether I should make mention of the Saturday concert in front of his friends, so I kept quiet until he raised the topic.

"Did you enjoy the show?" he asked.

"Very much," was my simple reply.

"What did you think of the dancing?" came the question.

"Very good," I answered, remembering all the good-looking young men on the stage.

"Those girls were hot, hey!"

I didn't want him to know that I thought that the boys were even hotter, so I smiled and nodded. Obviously his focus was more on the girls in the show, rather than the boys.

"Are you sitting by yourself?" he asked, moving closer as though he were going to sit on the bench next to me.

"I'm just waiting for some friends," I replied, causing him to back off slightly. I could see the disappointment in his face, but I was constantly aware that his friends were with him. Perhaps had he been on his own, I might have encouraged him to sit. Just then Sarisha ran up and greeted him warmly.

"Hello," she said, sitting on the bench next to me. "Don't you want to join us?"

Now it was Morgan's turn to be confused. Should he accept the invitation or saunter off with his friends.

"It's OK thanks."

I think he could see the disappointment now in my face, but he chose to leave with his friends and they wandered off.

"Why didn't he want to stay?" asked Sarisha, looking confused.

"It's probably my fault. I think he wanted to sit and I basically rejected him, then you came along."

"Are you saying that it's my fault?"

"No! Nothing like that. I just find it odd for him to suddenly befriend me the way he has."

"Maybe he likes you," giggled Sarisha, "but if he does, I'll scratch your eyes out. I've begun to think he's quite cute."

"Cute!" I remarked, rather loudly. "So you fancy him, then?"

"Well, he's not unpleasant on the eye," laughed Sarisha, looking in the direction that Morgan was heading.

"But what did you mean, 'he likes me'?" I asked a little perplexed.

"Maybe he likes boys more than he likes girls," whispered Sarisha, with a glint in her eyes.

Immediately I burst out laughing. "You are joking aren't you? All he could do was talk about the girls he saw in the show."

She never answered, but we both sat under the shade of the tree, laughing at the idea. Friends of ours came up to us to ask what the joke was, but we couldn't tell them. This was our private joke.

At the second break during the day, Sarisha and I again gathered under the tree on the bench to eat our lunch.

"I wonder if there's cricket practice today. I'm sure that practices are on a Monday," I said aloud, almost as though to myself.

Sarisha turned to me with that same wicked glint in her eye.

"You rascal! Are thinking what I'm thinking?"

"And what might that be?" I asked casually.

"That you're thinking of staying after school to watch him?"

I giggled. She had correctly read my mind.

"Well if you stay," she continued, "so do I. I hate the game, but at least he's pleasant on the eye."

"But I thought you weren't interested in him because he hasn't got a brain, so you once said?"

"Listen to who is talking. You've got fewer brain cells than I have, but I still associate with you," she said, jabbing me in the ribs so that I laughed uncontrollably.

Morgan appeared in the distance and saw us sitting once more under the tree, but this time he didn't have his group of friends, as we called them. He seemed a little awkward and unsure whether he should approach us, but I waved to him and this gave him the impetus to approach.

"Do you want to join us?" I asked, patting the bench next to me to indicate that he should sit there, but instead he chose to sit next to Sarisha.

I watched as he stretched his long, slim legs out and leaned back against the upright of the bench. Sarisha became very animated in her conversation with him and I found myself feeling a little ostracised.

"Are you playing cricket this afternoon?" asked Sarisha.

I leaned forward to see his face when he answered.

"Yes. Why, do you want to come and watch?"

"Raj and I thought we might stay after school and watch for a little while…" commented Sarisha.

"…Only because we have nothing else to do," I quickly added.

Once I had said it, I thought it was the wrong thing to say as it might imply that we were desperate, or Morgan might construe it to mean that as a last resort we would come and watch him.

"We're starting at 2.30," Morgan said, "and should be finished by 5pm."

"That's fine," I replied, "because the last bus going our way leaves at 5.30 from the school gate."

Before our conversation got any further, Morgan spotted some of his gang and rose rapidly to leave.

"I think I'd better be going," he said and hurried away.

"Do you think that we're an embarrassment to him in front of his friends, Raj?" asked Sarisha, after Morgan was out of earshot.

"Looks like it. Maybe we don't actually need people like that in our lives."

"Do you think he's ashamed to be seen with us because we might be considered 'nerds' among his sporting friends?" asked Sarisha.

"Who cares what they think," I replied, indignantly.

However, whatever we thought of Morgan's rapid departure, we still remained adamant that we would attend his cricket practice in the afternoon. A certain something seemed to attract both of us to him.

That afternoon, Sarisha and I sat on the school grandstand, a place we would seldom be seen in, and waited for the cricket game to commence. Eventually, Morgan and his team mates strutted out onto the field looking like a washing powder advertisement. Their outfits were so white and they were made even whiter against the contrasting colour of their dark skin and the lush green of the grass on which they were going to play.

First they did a few exercises to limber up, while Sarisha and I joked about some of their efforts, and then they practised some batting and bowling in the cricket nets before coming onto the pitch to have a short game. Morgan noticed us by giving a subtle nod in our direction. Sarisha waved frantically, but no wave was forthcoming from Morgan. Obviously he didn't want to make our presence too obvious to his other friends.

"What do you think his scene is?" asked Sarisha.

"What do you mean?" I asked genuinely not understanding where she was coming from with this line of questioning.

"Well I don't know. He seems never to be around the girls, but then he also seems to be a lover-boy, the sort of thing that would attract the girls; then he comes up to you at the theatre and starts conversing with you, something he's never done in his life so do you think he knows that you're gay?"

"Meaning what?" I responded.

"I've told you before; maybe he's interested in boys, but he can't say so to any of his friends. You also know, I'm sure, what Indians usually feel about people being gay."

I looked across the field and watched Morgan, thinking about what Sarisha had just said, for a while before answering.

"No, I don't think so," I replied nonchalantly. "Look how manly he looks out there. Do you think that's a person who enjoys going out with boys?"

I wasn't sure whether I was just trying to convince myself that I was wrong in my estimations of him.

"Well, I'm going to find out," said Sarisha, cutting into my thoughts.

"What are you going to do, Sarisha?"

"Ask him out on a date."

"What!" I exclaimed. "You can't do that," I quickly replied. "Do you know how embarrassing that is for a girl to ask a boy out on a date? If people found out they might think that you were nothing more than a slut."

This reply was more out of panic than sincerity.

"Well thank you very much, if that's what you think of me."

"Of course it's not what I think of you, but rather what others might think; that's all that worries me. Girls shouldn't ask boys out on dates; it's the boy who should do it."

"Are you sure that you're not a little bit jealous, if I ask him out?"

"Not at all," I responded, angrily.

"I'm telling you, after the practice today, I'm going to ask him out on a date," stated Sarisha, boldly, without really taking cognisance of my reply.

Dark, grey clouds had started to build up as the afternoon progressed and the teacher in charge of the cricket decided to call it a day early, before a thunderstorm materialised.

"They're finishing. Come, let's go and catch the bus," I said, rising from my seat and beginning to head away from the sports field in a desperate effort to avoid speaking to Morgan.

"No wait! I want to speak to him," said Sarisha, halting me in my tracks. "Remember I said I was going to ask him on a date."

I thought this was now getting embarrassing, so I started moving towards the bus stop while Sarisha hovered, waiting for Morgan to appear. When I reached the bus stop, I turned and saw Morgan and Sarisha conversing and walking together towards me.

"Why did you rush off?" enquired Morgan when he neared me.

"I thought the bus was coming," I lied, sheepishly.

Sarisha gave a slight smile because she knew that I was lying and that I was probably becoming embarrassed.

"I asked Morgan if he would like to go to movies with me on Saturday afternoon," said Sarisha rather smugly, smiling broadly at me as she said it.

I ventured a look at Morgan, more as confirmation of this statement, but when he saw my look, he must have had another thought in his head, and possibly realised my envy, because he said, "Why don't you join us, Raj. The three of us can go together."

It was my turn to smile broadly, not because Morgan had asked me, but because the look on Sarisha's face was a picture. To say she looked shocked would be an understatement, but then I wasn't about to upset their date. I don't think that Sarisha expected Morgan to invite me to go along.

"Well, that's up to you two," I replied.

Morgan then looked at Sarisha for confirmation and I looked at both of them. Of course I would love to be in their company, but if it were not to be, then that wouldn't worry me, or so I convinced myself.

"I suppose so," answered a reluctant Sarisha, after a moment of hesitation.

"Then that's settled. We'll all go to movies on Saturday," said Morgan, rather triumphantly.

The bus arrived and Sarisha and I boarded it, having said goodbye to Morgan. As we found some seats, she said, "I could kill you!"

"It wasn't my idea," I said, grinning at her frustration. "If you really don't want me there, then just say so and I won't come along. I'll make some sort of excuse as to why I can't make it."

"How could you do that to me?" asked Sarisha, still spitting words out like a snake spitting poison.

All I could do was shrug my shoulders; after all it was Morgan who had suggested the three of us going to the cinema and not me.

The journey home was tense, to say the least. Sarisha hardly spoke and I realised that she must be in deep thought about Morgan and my possibly 'gate crashing' her date. When we eventually arrived at our destination, we alighted from the bus and although I said good bye to her, she chose to pretend she hadn't heard me.

However, throughout the remainder of the week, the three of us sat together quite often during our lunch breaks, but at no time did I say anything about cancelling my visit to the movies with Morgan and Sarisha.

CHAPTER 6

Saturday morning arrived and I arose to a bright, sunny day. I leapt from my bed, dressed and washed; ate my breakfast and readied myself for movies in the afternoon with Sarisha and Morgan. I had told my mother where I was going that afternoon and she had given me some pocket money to pay for movies and my bus fare to town and back. It had been decided that we would all meet in Grey Street, have something to eat and then head to the movie house.

At midday, I caught the bus, which was pretty full with women who were going shopping, and headed into the city. It was a slow hour's journey, stopping and starting to pick up and drop off people, but eventually we made our way into Grey Street and I alighted once we reached our agreed-upon place. Sarisha was already standing waiting for Morgan and me to arrive. When we saw each other, we hugged and greeted each other warmly. At this moment in time, I noticed that Sarisha was happy to see me, so I thought that perhaps she was no longer jealous at my being invited to join her and Morgan for movies.

"Where are we going to eat?" I enquired as the hubbub of traffic almost drowned out our conversation.

"There's a small restaurant around the corner from here that I thought might be pleasant," she replied.

We didn't have to wait long before Morgan arrived, looking good in a pair of denim jeans and a bright yellow T-shirt.

"You look bright like a canary," commented Sarisha, causing Morgan a little embarrassment as he looked down at his T-shirt.

"Do you think it's too bright?" enquired Morgan, looking at his T-shirt.

I could see that he was somewhat taken aback by her statement, so I countered it by telling him that I thought it was a lovely colour and that it suited him, to which he smiled broadly. I don't know whether his smile was as a result of the compliment, or whether it was because I had said it, but either way, his smile made me feel good.

We made our way around the corner from the bus stop to the small restaurant that Sarisha had mentioned earlier. It was clean, busy yet cosy and we found a table in one of the corners where we made ourselves comfy. As we weren't that hungry, we ordered toasted sandwiches and cold drinks, which soon arrived.

People were animatedly conversing at the other tables, probably all having been shopping and now enjoying a respite for lunch.

"By the way, what film are we going to see?" asked Morgan.

"Good question," I commented. "I didn't even give it any thought as to what was showing."

"You have a choice," smiled Sarisha, the keeper of all knowledge; "The Bridge on the River Kwai or Tarzan goes to India."

Both Morgan and I burst out laughing.

"Are you serious?" I asked, in between giggles at the thought of seeing Tarzan going to India.

Sarisha grinned and nodded. "I'm very serious!"

"What's the Bridge film about?" enquired Morgan.

"I think it's about the Japanese and the Second World War," replied Sarisha.

"No I don't think I want to see a war film," he replied. "If that's all we have to choose from, then I think I'll have to go for Tarzan."

"I agree," I echoed, mainly because I didn't want to see fighting and war, and also it was because Morgan had chosen to see Tarzan, not that I was a Tarzan fan.

So it was agreed. We would endure Tarzan's journey to our mother country. I say mother country because that was where all our ancestors came from. The only reason we were living in South Africa was because many years before our parents were born, their ancestors were brought out to South Africa as labourers to work primarily on the sugar plantations.

Once we had finished eating and paid our bill, we made our way to the Shiraz Cinema in Victoria Street, where we paid and went in. Our eyes soon adjusted to the almost darkness of the venue and we found our seats, Sarisha going into the row first followed by Morgan and then me. This cinema was not like the theatre I had seen the variety concert in; in fact this place seemed like a dump. No wonder they kept the lights low, it was probably so that patrons wouldn't see the dirt.

We had each bought boxes of popcorn and bottles of Coca Cola to keep us nourished throughout Tarzan's journey through India, and soon the house lights dimmed even further and the first pictures of a documentary flickered onto the screen. The chatting came to a halt and we sat munching our popcorn, quietly observing the various scenes being shown on the screen. At the conclusion of the documentary, some sections of the audience, which, I think, were made up mostly of young people, applauded enthusiastically. Some adverts followed and it was during this period that I noticed Sarisha whispering into Morgan's ear, but was unable to make out what they were talking about. A cartoon then appeared on the screen and was followed by some trailers of forthcoming attractions and then it was interval.

"Will you two excuse me," said Sarisha, rising from her seat. "I need to go to the ladies room," she said, sliding passed us in the row.

The cinema lights had come up, illuminating the theatre to some extent. Morgan and I sat and chatted casually while Sarisha was away. Other patrons also left the auditorium, probably to have a smoke or get some fresh air, but we remained in our seats. As soon as she returned, she took over the conversation and dominated Morgan's attention. I didn't feel at all jealous with this, as I was just too happy to have him sitting next to me. After some time, the house lights dimmed again, people came scurrying back to their seats and a sense of excitement filled the theatre; the main feature was about to begin. Everybody seemed to get comfortable and we all sat back to enjoy Tarzan's mysterious journey through the jungles of India.

The film, which was in black and white, had been running for about fifteen minutes when I felt Morgan's knee gently touch mine. I never moved my leg but left it resting against his. He also never moved his, but out of the corner of my eye I could see that Sarisha had her hand on Morgan's left leg. I noticed that he never moved away from her clutches so I wasn't sure whether he liked both of us or whether he was just spreading his legs wide and had accidentally touched my leg. In the dark, I rested my elbow on the arm of the seat between Morgan and me and soon felt his elbow also rest against mine. Just like my leg, I left my elbow pushing up against his, and still he didn't remove it.

Tarzan continued to trundle on through the jungles of India, while Morgan's knee continued to rest leisurely against mine. While the audience giggled at the antics of the super-human ape-man, I noticed that Morgan had moved his left leg slightly away from Sarisha's clutches, and turned more towards my direction. I was, however, not about to make a grab at his leg like Sarisha had, but I did let his right leg rest heavily against mine.

Finally, Tarzan concluded his journey through India and to much applause from the audience, the house lights went up. As they did so, so Morgan and my legs parted their contact and the three of us rose from our seats, making our way out of the cinema.

"What should we do now?" asked Sarisha, when we emerged into the sunlit street, which still buzzed with people and vehicles.

Morgan looked at his watch and said that it was getting a little late and that he should be heading home. I could see the disappointment written across Sarisha's face, but I couldn't say that I blamed her. I enjoyed Morgan's company. After thanking Morgan for spending the afternoon with us, Sarisha and I made our way back to the bus stop and caught our bus home.

As we sat together on the bus, neither spoke of the 'contact' with Morgan in the cinema; neither wanted to admit to the other that they had found him attractive, nor that they had wished to have spent more time with him, alone.

The bus trundled along the road back to Phoenix, spewing out passengers, while at the same time gorging more as it travelled along the busy roads.

When I arrived home, my mother asked me to relate the whole film to her, making sure that I left no details out. Obviously I was not about to divulge Morgan's close proximity to either Sarisha or me, but I kept her entertained by Tarzan's antics.

"By the way, my child, there was a telephone call for you while you were out."

"Oh, who was it that called?" I enquired.

"A boy by the name of Peter. He sounded English, but I wasn't sure."

"Did he say what he wanted?" I asked, trying not to show too much excitement in my voice.

"No. He just said he would try again later."

For the rest of that night I waited in anticipation, but nothing materialised.

CHAPTER 7

Monday morning at school was no different from any other Monday morning, except of course, I waited to see Sarisha and ask her about the remainder of her weekend. Naturally I knew what her weekend was like as we'd spent part of it together at the cinema, but I wanted to know what emotions were going through her head as she laid her hand gently on Morgan's leg, in the dark.

When I saw her arriving, I rushed over to greet her, but in turn I received what might be construed as a cold shoulder.

"What's the matter?" I asked, looking puzzled.

"Nothing," came the curt reply, and she marched off towards her classroom to deposit her suitcase.

I followed – at a distance – and watched as she went into the classroom. I remained outside, watching through the window, but wasn't sure whether she knew that I was watching. At length, I sauntered closer to the classroom door and peered in.

"Sarisha, is anything the matter?" I hesitantly asked, before sidling closer to the doorway.

She was seated with her head cradled in her arms at her desk. She ignored my question, but still I advanced until I was inside of the classroom. I stood at the front of the room, staring at her.

"Please talk to me," I pleaded.

She gazed up at me and I could see tears welling up in her eyes.

"Please go away," she sobbed. "I don't want to talk about it."

I didn't move, but watched as she sobbed uncontrollably. Her head was laid on the desk and I saw her shoulders shaking as she cried. I walked over to her and put an arm around her shoulder, but she instantly shrugged free from my touch.

"Go away!"

"Sarisha, speak to me," I pleaded. "What's the matter?"

"You've hurt my feelings," she blurted, between sobs.

I suddenly realised that she must be talking about the cinema and what happened there in the dark between Morgan's leg and mine, but then how would she know?

"How did I hurt your feelings?" I innocently enquired.

"I like him," she blurted forth, "and I can see that he likes you better."

"How can you say that? How do you know he likes me more? Did you ask him?"

"I just know it. It's a woman's intuition," she sobbed.

"Don't talk rubbish," I answered.

"It's true," she continued. "We women know these things."

I wondered if women had been blessed with some inborn ability to read others' minds, or if she was just pretending to know such things.

"Well I didn't ask him to like me more than you," I volunteered, but this only made matters worse.

"It's not fair!"

"What's not fair?" I asked. "He went to the cinema with both of us and you had your hand on his leg. Did you see my hand on his leg? Of course not! So what is your problem?"

I realised that perhaps I had said the wrong thing about Sarisha having her hand on Morgan's leg, but it was too late; the words had come spilling out of my mouth.

"I just know that he likes you more," came her sobbing voice.

"You're being silly and in any case, I don't see the harm in both of us being his friend, Sarisha. So stop your crying and dry your eyes before someone sees you and then you'll have to explain to them."

She listened to what I said and immediately stopped her sobbing. The only sounds that emanated from her were her constant sniffs as she tried to prevent her nose from running.

"I don't want us to break up our friendship just because of a boy," I said, sitting down in the desk alongside of Sarisha and placing my hand on hers. "If you want him, take him."

"But I know he likes you," she sniffed.

"You have no proof of that and as I've said before, there's nothing to stop the three of us from going out together and being friends, so stop worrying."

Sarisha slowly took control of her emotions as a number of girls began to arrive at the classroom entrance and saw us sitting together. Both she and I rose and immediately left the classroom and made our way onto the playground, avoiding answering any enquiring questions from the girls as they entered the classroom. Out on the playground, Sarisha regained her composure and began to smile again, which made me feel better, that was, until she saw Morgan arrive. I noticed a pained look appear upon her face and then she hastily fled back in the direction of her classroom. I wondered if she was about to burst into tears once more. This time I chose not to follow; instead I made my way towards Morgan, after all, it was not me who had the emotional problems.

"Hi Morgan," I cheerily greeted as I neared him.

He smiled openly and returned the greeting. "How was your weekend?" he asked, slapping me across the shoulder in a very manly fashion, as he spoke.

"It was great, thanks. Well Saturday was great," I replied beaming broadly.

He beamed back and we stood grinning at each other, neither saying a word, much like two dumb-struck lovers. Thank goodness the school bell rang, breaking our stares at each other and we hastily headed towards our different classrooms. As I entered mine, Sarisha said, "I saw you talking to Morgan; did he say anything about Saturday?"

"Not a word," I replied, as I ventured towards my desk.

She glared at me as if to say I was lying.

"We didn't say anything," I reassured her. I couldn't very well tell her that we only stood and stared at each other, because she would have thought us mad.

"He didn't say anything about the cinema?"

"Nothing."

I think she could see from my expression that I was telling the truth because she suddenly dropped the subject.

The rest of the day was pretty uneventful and neither Sarisha nor I saw Morgan during the day.

CHAPTER 8

"Aunty Selvie, how old are you today?" enquired the young Krishna as he bounced on Aunty Selvie's knee.

I waited to hear her answer and knew that she was watching my every reaction.

"My darling, you shouldn't ask a lady her age, it's not polite," she replied, smiling sweetly at my little brother.

"Why is that Aunty Selvie?" I blurted out, before Krishna had a chance to ask the same question.

"It's just not done, my darling. Ladies never reveal their age."

"But men do," I retorted.

She laughed.

"We ladies must remain an enigma to you men."

"What's that?" I asked.

"It means we must remain a mystery to men," she replied, with a twinkle in her eyes.

"What good is that?" I continued. "If you remain a mystery then you will never find a man."

"But I found Uncle Harry," she smiled.

I could see the happiness in her face as she said his name. She had obviously decided not to remain a mystery when she had met him and by doing so, she married him.

"You love him very much, don't you?" I said, looking deeply into her eyes.

She smiled once more, almost glowingly.

"Of course I do, Raj, and one day you too will find someone that you love just like I and Uncle Harry love each other.

I scoffed at this thought. Love wasn't something at the top of my 'to do list' in life. Sure I would like to be attracted to someone, but I wasn't so sure about the 'love' thing.

"Have you met anyone nice?" enquired Aunty Selvie.

"I have some friends," I replied, without committing any further details.

"And is there any one that you like more than the others?"

This was something I had never given much thought to. I didn't judge my liking of people on a scoring chart like football, rugby or cricket. This was a difficult question.

"I don't see my liking of people by degrees of comparison; rather I like them or I don't. It is either black or white, without there being any grey areas," I answered having considered her question.

As I thought about this, it struck that I had mentioned the two words which seemed to be the bane of every South African's life: Black or White. I realised what I had said, but it didn't seem to worry Aunty Selvie.

"When you are a little older you will understand, Raj, but in the meantime, you sound very mature for a young man."

Aunty Selvie lifted Krishna from her knee and set him on the floor; rose from where she was sitting and entered her well-fitted lounge, leaving Krishna and me on the tiled veranda.

Inside of the lounge sat my mother and father, Uncles Harry and Sivan, Aunty Ashra and about five friends of Aunty Selvie's, including a White man, whose name was Mr. Walters. They were all here for Aunty Selvie's birthday to celebrate her unknown age. The drinks were flowing and there was much jollification and laughter as well as heated discussions. I remembered Aunty Selvie's earlier comment about it being fine for Indians and Whites to socialise while the sun shone, but I wondered what would happen to Mr. Walters when the sun set.

Most of the time, we children played outside, but as the afternoon progressed and early evening was arriving, we moved indoors and I took it upon myself to sit cross-legged on a rug in a corner of the lounge to listen to the adults' converse. We didn't often have many visitors at our house, so to see so many people together was an occasion for me. The conversations seemed to be of a very topical and of a general nature; nothing that I couldn't misunderstand. I noticed how Mr. Walters seemed to be almost subdued on occasions, but then I wondered if it had something to do with him being White and it getting dark outside.

The sun had set and the lights in the lounge illuminated the room brightly. Aunty Selvie had arranged dinner for everyone and after the children had been fed; those who were very young were taken off to one of the bedrooms and put on the beds to sleep. I however, continued to remain in the lounge with the adults.

At one stage my mother suggested that I join the other children in the bedroom, but Aunty Selvie intervened and said I could remain in their company.

Listening to the adults talk was like an education to me; far more interesting to me than what I learned at school. As the evening progressed, I heard topics of a social, entertaining and political nature being discussed and it was during these latter conversations that Mr. Walters seemed to come out of his shell, so to speak. I heard him speak vociferously about the injustices of the Apartheid government and how wrong it was to treat people differently. As I sat listening, I wished that Peter could have been here to hear these conversations and for me to discuss them with him, but that was not to be. I wondered how it was possible for a White man to be so open in his political conversations, but I saw no resentment from any of the people seated there in Aunty Selvie's lounge. After some time, I couldn't refrain from speaking. I had been quiet all night, listening, but now I had an urge to speak and question.

"Mr. Walters," my voice quavered, "May I ask a question?"

There was an immediate stunned silence as this child-like voice cut through the adults' talk and everyone's attention was drawn to me.

"What is it young man?" he asked, turning his attention to me.

"Will the police come and arrest you here because it is dark?"

Once again there was a stunned silence as each adult took in what I had said. Immediately my mother's face was a picture of horror; had I embarrassed her or had I said the wrong thing and in public?

"I hope not," came his friendly reply, "So long as you don't tell them."

The atmosphere had been broken and everyone burst out laughing, but I sensed it was a nervous laugh rather than a hearty one.

"I think it is time for you to go to sleep, Raj," said my mother rather sternly.

I then felt embarrassed because it seemed like a reprimand rather than an instruction. I could see that Aunty Selvie's reaction seemed different from my mother's. She obviously knew what I was trying to infer.

"Let him sit a little longer," she said, pleading with my mother, "after all, it is my birthday."

My mother relinquished and I was able to continue listening to the adults' conversations. As their talk resumed, Mr. Walters moved closer to where I was sitting.

"Raj, do you have any White friends?" he asked.

I looked embarrassed because I wasn't sure whether I should admit to this or not.

"Well, do you?"

I nodded.

"Yes sir," I quietly answered.

"At your school, perhaps?" he asked.

"No. I'm at an Indian school. There are only Indian children there. There are no other children."

He knew that I meant other children of colour.

"Do you see your White friends often?" he continued.

I was now becoming more and more embarrassed because I was afraid that the other adults would be listening and would start asking as to where and how I had come to make White friends.

I shook my head, but I think the pleading look in my eyes must have alerted him to my embarrassment, so he stopped asking questions about my White friends.

"I don't think it's wrong to have friends of other colours," he said, lighting up a cigarette. "I have known your aunty and uncle for many years now and we get on very well together, don't we Selvie?"

"What's that?" enquired Aunty Selvie, who had been interrupted in a conversation with Uncle Harry.

"I was telling Raj that we had known each other for many years."

"Oh yes," beamed Aunty Selvie.

I wondered where Aunty Selvie and Uncle Harry had met Mr. Walters for them to have known him for so long, but I was not about to find out.

"Raj," spoke my mother once more. "Why don't you go to the kitchen and get yourself a mineral or a tumbler of juice."

I knew from the tone of her voice that this was not an invitation, but rather an instruction, whether I was thirsty or not. I rose from my seating position on the floor and headed to the kitchen. I poured some juice into a tumbler and as I made my way back to the lounge, I heard my mother telling Aunty Selvie that she didn't think it was right for a child like me to listen to adult conversations, especially if they concerned politics.

"I think he's old enough to learn about what is happening in this country of ours," Aunty Selvie replied. "You can't let him grow up being like the ostrich that buries its head in the sand and hopes the problems of the world will go away. I think you underestimate your son's intellect," she continued.

I stayed hidden from the adults as I continued to listen to their debate about my being allowed listening to political talk.

"I think it's good for young people to debate politically," said Mr. Walters. "They need to be made aware of their situation while they are young," he resumed.

"That's all very well for you to say that; you're one of the privileged people in this land. You are not discriminated against like we are," said my mother.

I was stunned by her remark and expected an outburst from the others, but it never happened. Instead, Mr Walters quietly replied that, "You seem to forget that I am as much in danger being here tonight as you are, even though I am White. You realise that I can be arrested for being in the home of a non-White, and that I too am basically told where I can and cannot go, what I can and cannot read or do, because I am not party to the ideologies of the ruling powers in this country."

A deathly hush overcame the lounge and I hesitated cautiously outside of the lounge without any of the adults seeing me. I then heard Mr. Walters heave a sigh and suggest that he should be making his way home, so I scurried back into the kitchen. I heard Aunty Selvie and Uncle Harry's voices as they escorted Mr. Walters out and then heard my mother suggest to my father that they should also be going home. Once Mr. Walters had been seen off, and Aunty Selvie had returned to the lounge, she suggested to my mother and father that as the children were sleeping, to let them stay the night rather than awaken them, and also suggested that I might like to stay with my siblings. I of course became excited because I enjoyed her company and pleaded with my mother, who happily relinquished and she and my father set off for home.

Once the other guests had also departed and we had cleared the lounge of ashtrays filled with smelly cigarette ends, and taken all the glasses through to the kitchen, Uncle Harry said that he was off to bed.

Aunty Selvie poured herself a last drink and offered me something to drink, which I refused, and then settled down on the sofa with her feet tucked under her.

"Come and sit next to me, my darling," she said, patting the large cushion alongside of her.

I made my way to her and sat down.

"Now," she whispered, "Tell me about your White friend."

I looked surprised, as I had never mentioned Peter to anyone, other than Sarisha and I knew that she had never told anyone.

"I heard you talking to Mr Walters," she continued. "Now, where did you meet him and is he a nice boy?"

"How do you know that it's a male friend?" I enquired.

"I suspected that it might be as you told me you didn't have a girlfriend yet," answered Aunty Selvie.

I was surprised at how attentive Aunty Selvie was, but I also knew that I could trust her; so telling her was not embarrassing or awkward.

"I met him at a party," I replied.

"And what's his name? I'm assuming he has one!"

I laughed happily.

"Of course he has one; it's Peter."

"And how old is Peter?"

"He's a little older than me and I met him one night when I went to a party."

"I take it your mother knows nothing of this?"

I looked shocked, so she fully understood my meaning.

"You have nothing to fear, my darling; your secrets are my secrets."

Aunty Selvie then became like an information-seeking missile. She targeted me with question after question: where did he go to school? Where did he live? Did his parents know about me? What interests did he have? How often had we seen each other? I fielded each question, but then she threw a curved ball at me, much like I had seen Morgan bowl at cricket.

"Has he been to your house or you to his?"

I fell silent. I couldn't tell her that we had spent a night together at our house. My parents still had no idea that I had brought Peter home and I wasn't about to divulge my secret.

She smiled sweetly at me, patted my hand, which rested on the couch next to her, and said, "You have nothing to fear, I'll not mention this to your parents, my little darling."

This quiet acceptance puzzled me. When in my own home, I was always interrogated for information, and although Aunty Selvie had done much the same now, I didn't feel that the intention was the same as it was in my home. I had heard the word 'liberated' before and wondered if it referred to Aunty Selvie. If she was liberated, maybe that was why she and Mr. Walters got on so well. Maybe it had something to do with one's education that one could be liberated. Whatever it was, I felt really safe with Aunty Selvie and knew that any secrets I might have would remain just so, if she knew of them.

"Do you like this Peter?" she enquired, still patting my hand.

"I'm not sure, but I think I do." I hesitated for a moment, and then the floodgates opened.

"We also went to the beach together," I continued. "It was such a beautiful day and just the two of us being together made it even more beautiful."

"Which beach did you go to?"

"The one north of the Snake Park," I replied, "where the sand dunes and the bushes are."

"You must be careful there, Raj, because people can hide in the bushes and maybe attack you, especially if you are with a White boy."

"Why would they do that?" I asked innocently.

"Oh, you never know. There are those who hide in the bushes to rob for money and then there are those who just dislike seeing White people with people of other colours, and I wouldn't want either you or Peter to be attacked for any reason."

"I'm sure that Peter would protect me should we be attacked," I answered.

"Don't be too sure. Peter might try to protect you, but if your attackers are adults, they may be stronger than both of you."

"But I don't understand why people don't like others who are not of the same colour as themselves," I bemoaned.

"My darling, unfortunately, it is not usually the children who see the difference in colours, but rather it is the adults. We are the ones who have grown up in the Apartheid era and it is only through our talking to you children that you become aware of it. Some people grow up assuming that this is how it should be and therefore do nothing about it, while there are others who constantly try to undermine the system to bring about change, and often it is those people who suffer the most in their efforts to effect change."

"Aunty Selvie?" I asked, staring straight into her deep eyes. "Which of those people are you?"

She giggled.

"Raj, you surprise me by asking that question. I thought you would have known. I want change so that we might all benefit and not just some people. I like to mix with people of all colours because it is their brains and intellect that interests me and not the colour of their skin."

"I thought so," was all I could say, smiling heartily at her as she beamed back at me. "But tell me, where did you meet Mr. Walters?"

"We studied together at university."

"Were you friends?"

She smiled at me.

"Yes," came her whisper.

"Close friends like Peter and me?"

Again she smiled sweetly at me.

"You could say that, but I couldn't marry him because of the colour of his skin."

"So you married Uncle Harry instead."

"Oh, you mustn't see it like that. I met Uncle Harry after I had left university and we fell in love, but deep down inside of me, I still had good feelings for Mr. Walters, so we remained friends."

"Did Uncle Harry know about you and him?"

"Yes, I never kept anything from your uncle and he knows that Mr Walters and I are only friends."

"He seems a nice man, Mr Walters."

"Yes he is and it's nice to see him on occasions."

I felt good inside of me because both Aunty Selvie and I had shared a secret to each other and this seemed to bond us closer together, but I was also beginning to realise from what she had said to me that in my youth I had grown up in innocence, and it was through the adults that we young children were developing prejudices.

CHAPTER 9

My evening spent at Uncle Harry's and Aunty Selvie's proved beneficial for me in the sense that I now had a confidant in whom I could share secrets and I was sure that she felt better for having told someone other than Uncle Harry about Mr. Walters. Of course, this didn't mean that I had relinquished my relationship with Sarisha; on the contrary, I still confided in her and told her all my secrets.

At school, following the weekend, I told Sarisha about spending time at Aunty Selvie's, but I never mentioned anything about Mr. Walters or Aunty Selvie's relationship with him. Sarisha spent most of her time talking about Morgan. I actually thought it strange that I had not given Morgan a thought all weekend, but had rather spoken about Peter, who in fact I had not seen for quite a long time. I decided that Monday afternoon, after school, I was going to find a telephone call box and give Peter a call.

After school, and before the bus arrived, I ran down the street to the first call box I could find and dialled Peter's number. The phone rang three times before being answered by a female voice. 'Idiot', I thought as I replaced the telephone 'He won't be at home yet.' I thought of waiting to allow him time to get home from his school, and catching a later bus home, but then I thought Sarisha might question me as to why I wasn't going straight home. As I stood contemplating my dilemma, I noticed how a wind had struck up and that heavy grey clouds that had been looming overhead for some time seemed to be looking for a spot to drop their contents. I felt a few drops of rain followed by some heavier ones, and then the heavens opened. I rushed back to the phone booth and took shelter there as the rain began to pour down. An icy coldness surrounded me although I was in the confines of the musty, stale-urine- soaked telephone booth. I stood shivering, hugging myself in order to keep warm, and smelling the stale odour. The noise of the rain as it pelted the roof of the phone booth was deafening. As I peered out through the glass sides of the booth, I saw children scurrying in all directions to get to shelter; I even saw Sarisha making for a bus shelter to get out of the rain. As I stood and watched the falling rain, I noticed a person scurrying towards the booth. The door was flung open and a rain-drenched body entered, breathing heavily from the run.

"Morgan! What are you doing here?"

Morgan had entered my space and we were now cramped together in the small telephone booth, shivering.

"I saw you in here and so I thought I'd join you out of the rain," he gasped, trying to catch his breath. "Phew! This place stinks."

I felt a little embarrassed by our close proximity in such a public place and the smell, but it was not my doing; at least we were out of the rain.

"Were you using the phone?" he enquired.

Without thinking, I replied that I had tried to make a call.

"Oh, were you trying to phone home?"

"No, I tried to get hold of a friend," I replied, feeling his breath close to me.

"Who?" he asked.

I wasn't sure that I should tell him. After all, I wasn't sure whether he had any White friends and it might seem strange to him that I should know and have a White friend in the form of Peter.

"Just a friend," I answered.

He smiled. I wasn't sure whether the smile signalled his wondering if it was a girl or boy, nor did I know whether his smile was simply a friendly gesture, but I wasn't about to elaborate on Peter to him.

The rain continued its cascading, hitting the roof of the booth in a noisy fashion, while Morgan and I huddled together.

"Have you been keeping well?" asked Morgan.

"Yes thanks," I replied, glancing through the glass sides of the booth to see if anyone had seen us together in the booth.

"I've missed seeing you lately."

I didn't know how to respond to that statement, but smiled at Morgan.

"I like your company," he continued.

Once more I smiled, probably blushing at the same time.

"Its getting cold in here," said Morgan, hugging himself to stay warm.

I agreed and also hugged myself. We stood staring at each other as though waiting for someone to make a first move at what, I don't know. Morgan shuffled closer to me and stood with his shoulder touching mine. Immediately the close bodily contact sent a warm feeling through me and I soon began to feel warm inside. Whether this was purely psychological, I don't know, but it certainly made me feel good inside. We stood like this for what seemed like an eternity until the rain began to dissipate. The glass in the telephone booth began to steam up from our gathering warmth inside, in comparison to the coldness outside and the urine smell also seemed to increase with the warmth. Soon we were steamed up so much that it was difficult to see out. I felt our fingers touch and I tensed. Neither of us looked at the other, but continued to stare at the steamed-up glass. A tingling ran through my body as I felt his hand touch mine, but no sooner had that happened, than Morgan broke contact and said, "I think the rain's stopped," and opened the telephone booth door. We both spilled out onto the rain-drenched road, just as other children came out from their shelters. Neither spoke as we emerged, but there seemed to be a hidden glow between us. I wasn't sure whether Sarisha had noticed us emerging together from the phone booth, but she never said anything to me.

During the rest of the week at school, Morgan and I crossed paths on a number of occasions, but nothing of the telephone booth was mentioned.

On Thursday afternoon, I was again headed towards the telephone booth and made a call to Peter's number. This time, he answered.

"Hello, Peter?"

"Yes!"

"Hi, it's Raj here. How are you?"

"Oh hi! I'm fine thanks and you?"

"I'm also well."

There was a pause of silence.

"I tried to phone you earlier in the week, but realised that you wouldn't be home from school yet."

There was another moment of silence.

I wondered whether I had done the right thing by phoning him now. The awkward silence continued for a while.

"I was wondering whether you were doing anything on Saturday, because if not, would you like to meet me somewhere and perhaps we could do something."

"I'm not sure," came the reply.

That answer confused me a little. Did he mean he wasn't sure what he was doing or wasn't sure whether to meet me or not? There seemed to be something strange in Peter's voice. It didn't sound like the Peter I had first met, but I wasn't about to give up trying.

"Maybe we can go to the beach or a movie?" I suggested.

"I don't know if I'll be able to make it," was Peter's answer to my suggestion.

Again a moment of silence occurred.

"Well, if you have a change of heart, please give me a call. Will you do that?"

"Sure. Thanks for the call," was all he said, and the phone then went dead.

At no time during our short conversation had Peter referred to my name, so I wondered if there was someone else with him at the time and he was embarrassed to mention my name. I also wondered why he had seemed so distant in our conversation. Maybe I had expected too much from him, but I had only phoned because I hadn't spoken to him for some time and wanted to know if he was well. I walked aimlessly away from the phone booth, feeling somewhat down-hearted at the 'rejection' I had received from Peter, but I soon stopped feeling sorry for myself and set off home.

On Friday, during school assembly, Sarisha sent me a note asking if I would like to attend a party on Saturday evening. I quietly opened the note while the headmaster droned on in his own subliminal way – none of us ever knew what he was talking about – and read its contents. I tried to catch her eye while the short, rotund headmaster droned on. At length, we made eye contact and I smiled and nodded, indicating that I would like to attend.

"Naidoo, R, you are not paying attention to what I am saying," boomed a voice from the front of the school hall.

I swung my attention to the direction from which the sound emanated and saw the headmaster staring at me over the top of his thick glasses. His beady little eyes, which were normally magnified through his thick lenses, seemed to burrow through my brain and I waited to hear if he was going to say anything more to me. The entire assembly suddenly awoke from their hypnotic state and heads turned in search of my face.

"Naidoo, R, if you have no interest in what I have to say, make your way to my office immediately and wait for me there."

I stared back in horror at his instruction. However, he was right; I really had no interest in what he had to say so slowly I made my way from the hall and exited to await this little man's arrival.

As I stood in the corridor outside of his office, the secretaries looked at me in surprise. This was the first time that I had ever been sent to the headmaster's office. Some even asked why I was outside the headmaster's office. Eventually the assembly came to an end and I heard everybody leaving the hall. Along the corridor waddled Mr. R.K Govender, our headmaster. He opened the door to his office and ordered me in. Once I was in, I closed the door behind me and he made his way to behind his desk, removing his academic gown as he did so. He hung his black gown on a hat stand that stood in a corner near his desk, and then seated himself. Once more the beady eyes peered over the top of his glasses.

"Naidoo, R, who were you talking to during assembly?"

"No one, sir," I answered, knowing that I hadn't been talking.

"Don't lie, boy, I saw you."

"Sir, I never spoke to anyone."

"Naidoo, R, there is one thing that I cannot tolerate from a person and that is a person who tells lies. To me they are the lowest form of humanity."

"I quite agree with you sir, but I didn't speak to anyone, sir."

"But I saw you. You disturbed my concentration on what I was saying in assembly," he replied, now looking through his glasses at me.

His eyes suddenly became magnified and I wanted to laugh when I saw his bulging eyes staring at me.

"Sir, I am not lying to you. I didn't speak; I only nodded my head."

"Well, there you go; you did something," he replied with glee like someone catching someone else red-handed.

"But I wasn't speaking, sir. In fact, I never made any sound whatsoever."

"You disturbed me, boy and for that you should be punished."

"Sir, I cannot see how I should be punished if I nodded my head without making any sound. It was because I was tired sir and I was nodding off."

Now I knew I was entering the realm of lies.

"So my speech was boring, is that what you're saying?"

"No sir, you're saying that."

"Don't be insolent, boy."

"I'm not, sir, but you said that your speech was boring, not me."

"Do you know, Naidoo, R, you remind me of your aunt. She too was cheeky when she was younger, but I think that her husband has drilled that out of her now."

"And which aunt might that be, sir?"

"Your Aunt Selvie."

The minute that he mentioned her name, I came to her defence.

"I don't think Aunty Selvie is either rude or cheeky, sir, and I know for certain she would never allow another person to drill, as you put it, anything out of her, least of all her husband. She is an independent woman who has a sharp brain and it is her determination and forthrightness that I respect more than anything else in her. It shocks me to think that you see her as being cheeky, and I'm sure that it would shock her to know that you feel that way about her. However, she is such a dignified lady that she would probably tell me to take it from whence it comes if I had to mention this conversation to her."

Mr. R. K. Govender merely stared silently in disbelief at me as I spoke. I could see his cheeks beginning to puff up in anger as I spoke. When I had finished talking, he simply pointed to the door of his office and said, "I think you'd better leave."

I thanked him for the conversation, opened the door, closed it behind me and as I wandered down the corridor from his office, a wry smile emerged across my face. I wish Aunty Selvie had been there to hear me. I'm sure that she would have been very proud of the way I stood up for her. In fact, I was a little shocked by the way I had spoken up in her defence. I realised I was growing up, mentally.

CHAPTER 10

The party that Sarisha had alluded to in her note in assembly was to be held in Chatsworth, which was quite a way from where we lived, but she had assured me that we could get a lift with another friend of hers, so all I had to do was ask my mother if it would be fine with her for me to attend the party.

"But Amah, Sarisha is also going and all our friends from school are going to be there."

"Yes my child, I know about Sarisha, but I do not know these other friends and I wouldn't want you smoking or drinking and getting into trouble."

"But Amah, I don't smoke," I replied.

"And drink?" she asked, with a raised eyebrow.

"Hm! Not really."

"I take it that 'not really' means, yes!"

I hung my head slightly because I knew how my father's drinking upset my mother, but didn't deny it.

"Only the occasional beer, Amah," I answered in a hushed tone.

"OK, but don't tell your father; you know what he's like."

I hugged her and thanked her profusely and then rushed to my room to see what clothes I might put out to wear that evening. Once I had selected my outfit, I rushed down the road to Sarisha's house to tell her.

At seven that evening, I went down to Sarisha's house once more and we waited for our lift to arrive. We hadn't waited long when a ramshackle Zephyr car arrived with a male driver behind the wheel. We both climbed in and Sarisha introduced me to the driver, whose name was Alvin and who looked about twenty. Sarisha sat in the front next to Alvin while I sat in the rear. Every now and then I noticed Alvin looking at me in the rear-view mirror, perhaps wondering who exactly I was, just like I was doing about him. He looked a cross between an Indian and a White because he seemed much lighter in skin colour than Sarisha and me, but not as white as Peter. As we drove along the road, heading towards Chatsworth, I wondered where and how Sarisha had got to know Alvin because I had never heard his name mentioned before. However, I did notice that Sarisha spent most of the journey smiling sweetly at the concentrating Alvin. I wondered whether Sarisha had him as a boyfriend on the quiet and if so, I wondered why she had not said anything to me; after all, we did share our secrets with one another.

We eventually arrived at the party venue and alighted from the battered Zephyr.

"Where do you know Alvin from?" I whispered as we emerged from the car.

"I'll tell you later," she whispered back.

Alvin climbed out and locked the car, then led us up to the front door of the house where the party was being held. Before we even arrived at the front door, the loud music could be heard, 'Thump! Thump! Thump! It almost made the glass windows of the house vibrate it was so loud. We knocked on the door, but to no avail, so Alvin tried the door handle and the door opened. A blast of music hit us as we crossed the threshold into the warm confines of an elegantly decorated house. In many respects, it reminded me of Aunty Selvie and Uncle Harry's house. As we entered and closed the front door behind us, a young man of around Alvin's age appeared.

"Hi my friend," said the young man, clasping Alvin's hand and shaking it.

The young man introduced himself to Sarisha and me as Henry. He too was light-skinned like Alvin, slightly stocky in build and with a charmingly broad smile, when he smiled.

We were escorted into the lounge area which seemed to be overflowing with bodies scattered all over the place, while the music continued to beat out its rhythmic thumps!

"The bar's in the kitchen and so is the food; so make yourselves at home and get a drink," invited Henry, and then disappeared to mingle among the crowd.

Alvin volunteered to get us each a drink and then disappeared in the direction of the kitchen, leaving Sarisha and me to be deafened by the constant blast of the music.

"Tell me about Alvin," I asked, when he had disappeared.

"I met him in one of the Tea Rooms I went into in Grey Street one Saturday morning. He was working behind the counter and we started to talk to each other, and you know, one thing led to another and soon he asked me out."

"You mean you've been out with him before and never told me!"

"No, this is the first time that I've been out with him. That's why I wanted you along as well."

"Oh, to keep an eye on you."

"If you put it like that, yes. But I also thought you might like to go out for a change."

"Do you know anyone else here?"

Sarisha looked around the lounge area then shook her head.

"Me neither, and I told my mother that all our school friends were going to be here," I said, feeling a little guilty at the lie I had told her.

There were some people dancing in the lounge to the sound of the music, but most seemed to be content to stand or sit around and chat to one another. Alvin soon reappeared with our drinks, a beer for each of us, and began to chat happily to Sarisha, who readily enjoyed the attention she was receiving from him. After a while of standing like a forlorn orphan or outcast, I chose to wander around the lounge and then into some of the other rooms in the house, just to see how the 'other half' lived. As I progressed down a long corridor from the lounge, it struck me that the people who owned this house must be financially well off. Along the corridor wall was a collection of beautiful pieces of artwork. There were what I would call traditional paintings like the kind you might find in an art gallery – landscapes and paintings of bowls of fruit and flowers – not really my style. Then I caught sight of one, which caused me to stop and stare. It wasn't a painting, but rather a tile: a ceramic tile, framed in a glass. It had a three-D effect to it and it resembled a cowry shell, but its beauty came in the various colours it created. I stood and looked at it admiring its changing hues, because whenever you moved, the colours seemed to change from blues to purples to greens and deep reds.

"Do you like that?" a voice said behind me.

"I think it's beautiful," I replied, turning to see who was speaking to me.

"I like it too," said the voice.

I turned to be confronted by Morgan.

"Hi!" I said looking surprised at seeing him there. "What are you doing here?"

"I was invited to the party," he answered.

I beamed at seeing him and we stood grinning at each other.

"Do you know these people?" I ventured.

"Henry's my cousin," he replied.

I know I must have looked very surprised by his comment, because he quickly added, "My Dad's sister is married to Henry's father."

By this I knew then that his aunty was Indian but his uncle was 'half-cast' or as they were called, Coloured, and that is why I thought Henry was the same.

"But what are you doing here?" asked Morgan.

"Sarisha was invited by Alvin. I don't know if you know him."

Morgan nodded that he did, but from the expression on his face, I thought that maybe he didn't like Alvin, for some reason.

"I think that they're going out together," I continued.

Morgan's expression seemed to become more severe.

"Why do you look at me like that?"

"It's none of my business, but I think she should think carefully about him."

"Why?"

"I just think that he's trouble."

I respected Morgan's views but wasn't sure that if I mentioned this to Sarisha that she would believe me; after all, they say that love is blind and at the moment, I think that Sarisha was completely unsighted.

"Do you want me to say something to her?" asked Morgan.

I seized at the opportunity and gladly accepted his invitation to deal with the potential confrontation that Sarisha would create.

"Would you mind? After all, I really like her and she is my best friend, so I wouldn't want her to be hurt," I answered.

"By the way, to get back to this art piece; do you know what it represents?" asked Morgan, pointing to the ceramic tile.

"No," I answered.

"It's life," he replied. "You see the centre, that's our birth and then as it spirals outwards, that's how we shed our inhibitions and spread our wings and journey in different directions."

I stood amazed at his knowledge, but then I wasn't sure whether what he was in fact telling me the truth; but it sounded right to me, so I believed his interpretation of the artwork. I moved slowly too and fro in front of the tile and watched how the light played with the metallic colours, changing as I moved – it was fascinating and almost hypnotic.

"Come," said Morgan, "Let's go and join the others."

My concentration on the beautiful tile was broken and we headed back down the corridor towards the lounge, where we found Sarisha happily dancing with Alvin. I watched both of them, wondering what Morgan had meant about Alvin being 'trouble'.

The music still had its incessant 'thump! thump!' and bodies were gyrating in time to the beat. I stood with my beer in my hand and watched the crowded lounge. Throughout this, it was obviously necessary to shout if one wanted to speak, in order to be heard above the noise. Most of what Morgan was shouting to me, I didn't hear properly, but it didn't seem to matter as it was just pleasant to know that I at least knew somebody at the party, other than Sarisha.

As the night progressed, I noticed that Morgan did, at one time, manage to get to talk to Sarisha alone, but what was actually said, I had no idea. I tried to fathom out what was being said by the expressions on their faces, but wasn't too successful.

"Did you manage to say something to her?" I asked when Morgan was near me at one stage and when the level of music noise had dissipated.

"Yes, but I don't think she was very interested in listening to me. She actually said that I was just jealous and wasn't really interested in listening to what I had to say."

I suppose I could understand why Sarisha might say that because she had previously had strong feelings for Morgan, but he chose to ignore those feelings and retain her purely as a friend.

It must have been close to midnight, when the sound of someone pounding on the front door of the house caused the DJ to turn down the music. Henry made his way to the front door and opened it. There standing on the doorstep were three burly White policemen. They spoke to Henry for a moment and then entered the house. As they came into the lounge area where we were all sitting, dancing and partying, a silence fell over the crowd. Apart from the sound of the music, one could have heard a pin drop. The presence of the White men in our midst caused some anxiety among us. The three policemen walked around the room, surveying each person there; glaring at us with disdain.

It was clear from their appearances that at least two were Afrikaans speaking men. I say that because at the time, most Afrikaans-speaking men chose to grow moustaches and this became a symbol of their identification. Generally, the English speaking Whites were clean-shaven. The third man didn't have a moustache, so I wasn't sure what his home language was, but assumed he would be English-speaking. It must be pointed out, that during this period in the country's history, although there was Apartheid among the colour groups, there was also an apparent difference in outlook and ideology between English-speaking and Afrikaans-speaking Whites.

The largest of the three policemen walked up to Sarisha, glared at her sitting with Alvin and asked what they were doing at this house.

"We're having a party," replied Sarisha, a little intimidated by these men.

The man never spoke again, but wandered around the lounge looking at everyone, presumably looking to see that there were no Whites among the non-Whites.

The fact that they were in uniform with revolvers by their sides and the fact that their looks intimidated us, we all became subdued and subservient.

The man without the moustache, on occasions, smiled at one or two of us, but it didn't endear us to them.

"Whose house is this?" boomed the voice of the largest man.

"It's my parents' home," said Henry, trying to sound assertive.

"Do you have a search warrant?" blurted Alvin, rising from where he'd been sitting with Sarisha.

The largest man swung round to focus his attention on Alvin.

"And who are you, you little shit!" he boomed, glaring at Alvin.

Alvin didn't seem fazed by the man's aggressive tone, but stood his ground. Sarisha tried to pull his arm to get him to sit down and be quiet, but Alvin shook her grasp from his arm.

"I asked you if you had a search warrant," continued Alvin. "You have no right to barge in here while we're having a private party like this and search us."

The policeman leered into Alvin's face.

"When did we say anything about a search, or have you got something to hide? You seem to have a lot to say for someone so young. Maybe we should take you down to the station and find out just what it is that you're trying to hide if you don't want us to search."

"Alvin, leave it," whispered Sarisha, trying to get him to calm down.

"They've got no right to barge in here like this," resumed Alvin, raising his voice.

The smooth-looking policeman advanced towards Alvin.

"Sir," he said, and we could hear that he was English-speaking, as he didn't have an accent so common among Afrikaans speaking people. "We only came here because we had a complaint about the excessive noise coming from this house. When we arrived, we could clearly hear the loud music blaring down the street. All we wanted was for you to tone down the noise."

"But you seem to want to cause trouble with us," reprimanded the largest of the policemen. "You four come with us!" he said, pointing to Alvin, Henry, Sarisha and me.

I panicked and asked why I was needed to go with them; after all, I hadn't said anything to provoke them. A policeman took each of us guys by the arm and led us out to their van, while Sarisha followed meekly. We were thrown into the back of the police van and the door was slammed shut and locked. We could see out through the thick wire mesh that covered the back of the truck, and therefore, just as we could see out, so people could see in. We were like animals in a cage.

The three policemen clambered into the front of the van and soon we sped off, the cold air breezing through the back as we huddled together. I didn't know where they were taking us or why, but I hoped that Morgan would at least have the insight to either follow us or find out where we were being taken so that we could at least get home afterwards, that is if we were to be released.

We drove through the darkened, empty streets until we eventually drove into the grounds of a police station. The vehicle came to a halt and the three policemen climbed out. The largest man unlocked the back door and we were led into the charge office where we stood waiting for something to happen.

The policeman behind the desk asked his colleagues why we had been brought in and what the charges were. Throughout, their conversations were conducted in Afrikaans, a language that all four of us could understand, so we were able to follow their train of thinking.

"Disturbing the peace, but this one needs the shit beaten out of him," replied the largest policeman.

"Why?" asked the man behind the desk.

"You know what these half-cast Coloureds are like – full of shit!"

"Have you had any other problems tonight?" asked the English-speaking policeman to his colleague behind the desk.

"There was only an incident when a White guy got caught having sex with a Black woman," came the reply in Afrikaans.

"And what did you do?" asked the English-speaking man.

"I just reprimanded them and sent them off," was the Afrikaans reply.

Immediately, on hearing this, my mind became confused. Here I was growing up in a country that practiced segregation and where it was a criminal offence to have sex with a person of another colour group, and added to that, I remembered what Aunty Selvie had told me about Whites and non-Whites being together after dark, yet here was a policeman allowing a Black and a White to do just that and letting them get off free, while we stood waiting the outcome of our future. I immediately decided that if we were to be thrown into jail, when we got to court, I would divulge this information about the man having sex with a Black woman.

The large Afrikaans-speaking policeman came to the front desk, glared once more at us and said we could go. I don't know whether he realized that we could understand what had been discussed in front of us, but it was a relief to leave the confines of his stuffy police station. As we exited the building, a set of car lights flashed at us. We hurried over to the car and found Morgan waiting for us. I was so pleased to see him in his car, waiting for us, that I could have flung my arms around him there and then. We all bundled into the vehicle and sped off back to Henry's house, where we dropped Henry and then made our way to our various homes.

I chose never to tell my parents of our adventure with the police, but it did open my eyes to the hypocrisy that was taking place in the country.

CHAPTER 11

A week after our episode with the police, the telephone at home rang on the Friday afternoon and my mother answered it.

"Raj, there's a call for you," she bellowed from the lounge as she returned to her work in the kitchen.

I made my way from my bedroom and picked up the receiver.

"Hello, Raj speaking."

"Hi Raj, it's Peter," came the reply, sounding sprightly and friendly, so differently from the last time that I had spoken to him.

"Hi Peter, how're things with you?"

"Great thanks. Listen, I'm sorry about the last time I spoke to you, but my Mom was next to the phone so I couldn't speak properly."

"Oh that's OK," I replied, relieved to know that I wasn't the cause of his depressed sounding voice. "I wondered if something was wrong, but I'm glad you phoned back."

"I was wondering if you were doing anything this weekend?"

"Why, what did you have in mind?"

"I wondered if you wanted to go to the beach again on Saturday."

"That would be great," I replied, without showing too much excitement in my voice. "Should we meet at the same place as last time?"

I could feel my heart pounding with excitement at the thought of Peter and me seeing each other again.

"What time should I meet you?"

"I should be there between 9:30 and 10:00. Just wait for me where you did last time," suggested Peter.

"I'm looking forward to that," I replied excitedly, as I said goodbye to Peter and replaced the telephone.

"Who was that?" shouted my mother from the kitchen.

"Just a friend," I cautiously answered, returning to my bedroom.

I think I floated to my room after having heard his voice on the phone and immediately packed my backpack with my swimming shorts and a towel, ready for the next day.

Friday evening, my father arrived home late and drunk. He'd been visiting a friend of his and they had obviously overindulged in the Cane Spirits or some such alcohol and he started verbally abusing my mother and me. My mother tried to pacify him and get him to go to bed, but he insisted on carrying on with his drinking, shouting that he needed another glass of something. My mother obligingly fetched a glass from the kitchen and poured a small tot for my father and then filled up the glass with water. When my father tasted the diluted drink, he erupted once more, cursing my mother and shouting at her to bring him the bottle. She timidly returned to the kitchen and brought the required bottle of Whiskey, which she handed to him. He poured the contents of his diluted drink into a pot plant that was standing nearby to him and refilled his glass with pure whiskey. I knew that the more he drank, the more aggressive he would become, so I ventured to my room and closed the door. I think my mother did likewise and went to her room because suddenly the house became quiet.

After some time of enduring silence, I ventured out of my room and found my father having passed out on the sofa in the lounge; the half empty bottle of Whiskey standing on the coffee table, opened, and his glass standing alongside of the bottle, untouched. I returned to my room, undressed, climbed into my bed and was soon fast asleep.

Early on Saturday morning, I tip-toed out of my room on my way to the bathroom and there in the lounge lay my father, snoring his head off while the alcohol stood where it had been left the night before. Before going to the bathroom, I picked up the Whiskey bottle and his glass and took them through to the kitchen, then went on my way to the bathroom. Having washed my face and brushed my teeth, I returned to my room and prepared for my journey to town and the beach. By 8:00a.m, I had greeted my mother, who had risen, told her I was going to town and had left to catch the bus.

My mother had given me a little money and I still had some of my own pocket money left, so I felt like a millionaire as I set off on my journey. The bus wasn't very full, except for a few elderly women on their way to market, so I was able to sit on my own and watch the passing scenery – that which might be construed as scenery. Once again, on arriving in the centre of Durban, I had to change buses in order to reach the beachfront, but this bus also seemed empty. As we neared the Snake Park beach area, I pressed the buzzer for the bus to stop and when it did, I alighted from it and crossed the road to the beach.

As I stood looking at the calm sea, I noticed a few surfers waiting patiently for a wave or two to develop, but without much success by the looks of things. While I was standing watching the surfers and waiting for Peter to arrive, a man of about thirty approached me and asked if I had a light for him.

"I'm sorry, but I don't smoke," I replied.

He smiled and apologised. I noticed that he wandered off to another person and asked the same question. This time he was successful. He then ventured back in my direction, happily puffing on his cigarette.

"I managed to get a light," he said, indicating his lit cigarette to me.

"So I see."

"Sure you wouldn't like a smoke?" he asked.

I grinned sheepishly and shook my head.

"You waiting for someone?" he asked.

I wasn't sure where his line of questioning was leading, so I wasn't sure whether I should tell him that I was waiting for Peter.

"Yes," I finally said, without elaborating on whom I was waiting for.

"A friend of yours, perhaps?"

"Yes," I chirped.

By this time I was sitting on the top of a low stonewall while he stood alongside of me. After having had a couple of puffs of his cigarette, he jumped up onto the stone wall and sat next to me, his leg barely touching mine. I didn't find this offensive so I left my leg where it was. I could feel a slight pressure being exerted on my leg from his and when I turned to look at him, I found him smiling at me.

"You're very good looking, you know," he said, continuing to smile at me.

I stammered, not knowing how to respond. If I was perfectly honest with myself as I looked at him, I had to admit that he wasn't bad looking himself, but I wasn't about to tell him that.

"Thank you," I eventually managed to squeak out of my voice.

I could feel his leg press harder against mine, so I shifted my seating slightly, moving my leg away from his in the process. As I did this, so he leapt from the stone wall and headed towards the men's toilet situated on the beach. As he was about to enter, he turned to face me and I noticed an ever so slight nod of his head as though he were beckoning me to follow him. Thoughts flashed through my head: was he going to rob me in there or was it some kind of trap, me being with a White man? I remained against the stone wall not knowing whether to flee the area or follow him out of curiosity. Fortunately for me, the sound of a motor bike came rushing to my aid – it was Peter.

"I'm so glad you're here," I gabbled as soon as Peter neared me.

"Why what's the problem? You look a bit stressed."

"Let's just go and walk along the beach," I responded, heading towards the Coloureds' beach away from the Whites' beach with Peter following at a slight distance.

"Why the hurry?" shouted Peter to me.

I turned to look back at where I'd been waiting for Peter and saw the man exit the toilet building and look around, obviously for me. I didn't stop, but kept my hurried pace with Peter now trotting to keep up. Once we were out of sight of the building, I slowed down to allow Peter to catch up to me.

"What's your rush, Raj?"

"There was a man pestering me back there, but fortunately you arrived in time. I just didn't want him following us."

"What was he doing to you to upset you like that?"

"I don't know."

"What do you mean you don't know?"

I wasn't sure whether I should tell Peter about the man's leg up against mine and his suggesting that I follow him.

"Well, don't worry, he's not following us," said Peter trying to reassure me.

We headed in the direction of the sand dunes where we had spent our other day at the beach and soon came to them. We headed inland up the sand dunes until we found our secluded spot with the mangrove bushes; threw down our towels and stripped off our clothes. Peter had on his Speedo under his shorts but my shorts were in my backpack. As I stood naked in the shade of some mangrove bushes, Peter smiled at me.

"You really have a cute body," he said, sitting on his towel watching me.

"Cute! What do you mean by cute?"

Peter giggled and replied: "It just is. Now put your shorts on before someone sees you."

I hastily pulled on my swimming shorts and lay down on my towel next to him. We ladled suntan lotion onto each other as we could already feel the intensity of the sun on our bodies. As we lay on the sand dune, the air was still and even the sounds of the waves seemed to be cut off from us, so much so, that we could whisper to each other and it sounded loud. In fact, it felt as if the whole world was cut off from us.

"So tell me what you have been doing lately," enquired Peter, turning to face me.

"Nothing much. Going to school and that's about it," I replied, smiling back at Peter's sun-tanned face.

"I don't believe you. Surely you've been around? Been to any parties lately?" asked Peter.

I froze with anticipation. Did Peter know of our party and the arrest and if so, how? Or was he just being interested in what I did?

"I went to a party recently with some friends from school," I said, without elaborating on what happened. "And what about you?"

"We had a school function last week and this week we had a fashion show at the school."

"And were you one of the models?" I jokingly quipped.

"As a matter of fact, yes."

"Ooh," I laughed. "I'd have loved to have seen that."

"I think I was actually very good."

"Well, you've got the face and the figure to be a successful model," I remarked.

"Thanks," answered Peter, smiling broadly. "Oh, and by the way, our school's going on a sports tour during the coming holidays, so I'm off to Cape Town for a week."

"Wow! Cape Town! I've never been there before. That sounds great, Peter. What sports are going to be played?"

"The girls' hockey team is going along with the rugby team."

"Are you in the rugby team?"

"Believe it or not, yes!"

"Well I hope you don't get hurt in any of your games."

Peter laughed and said that it was part of the game to get hurt; it was like the dirtier you got and the more scrapes and bruises there were on you, the better you had played. I didn't say anything, but I thought this to be a very naive outlook to have.

"Do you play any sport, Raj?"

"No, but I don't mind watching," I said, thinking of Morgan's cricket games. "I wouldn't mind watching you play rugby," I added.

"In that case you'll have to come to Cape Town and watch us there," joked Peter.

I knew that this idea was an impossible one as, not only could I not afford to go to Cape Town but if what the adults had said about Apartheid was true, how would I be allowed to go to a venue where Whites were playing sport without creating some sort of problem for the organisers?

"I'm actually looking forward to going on tour," continued Peter, "as my girlfriend is also going to be there. She's the captain of the girls' hockey team."

I think my face must have given my thoughts away. His girlfriend! He had never mentioned this before. When did she appear on the scene and what then was our relationship, I wondered?

"You have a girlfriend?" I enquired, as if I hadn't really heard what he'd said.

"Sure. We've been going out for about three weeks now."

"Oh … you didn't say anything like that before, that's why I was a little taken aback… I thought…"

"Raj, you don't have to worry. I still like you as a friend."

"But that night you spent at my house… how do you explain that?"

Peter became a little awkward and fidgety as he lay on his towel, looking at me and reminiscing the night we had spent together.

"Raj, you must try to understand that I like you very much, but I also like her as well."

"Have you slept with her like you did with me?"

"I don't think it's fair to ask me that, Raj. You must also understand that my family expects me to have a girlfriend."

"What do you mean your family expects you to have a girlfriend? That should be a choice of yours, not theirs."

"Raj, doesn't your family expect you to have a girlfriend and maybe marry her one day?"

I thought about this. Nothing like that had been discussed before. However, what Peter was saying was true amongst Indians, but I had never had the urge to feel for a girl in the way that I felt for Peter or Morgan. I kept quiet and I think that Peter could sense my disappointment at his mention of the girlfriend.

"Come, let's stop all this serious talk and go for a swim," suggested Peter jumping up and running to the top of the sand dune. "I'll race you to the water," he said and sped off in the direction of the sea.

I stood up and walked to the top of the sand dune where I watched as he frolicked in the waves. He shouted something to me, but I was unable to make out what he was saying. Then I saw him waving to me, so I waved back but remained on the peak of the sand dune, after all, I didn't want to leave our clothes in case someone came and stole them while we were swimming. As I stood there, I noticed a White man heading up towards the sand dune where I stood. As he neared, I recognised him as the man who had been speaking to me before Peter had arrived on his motor bike.

I remained on the dune watching both the man and Peter. When the man reached me he smiled and said, "So this is where you disappeared to."

I didn't respond as he stood next to me.

"Is that your friend down there?" he enquired, pointing to Peter.

I still didn't respond but moved back to where our towels lay. The man followed and on seeing the two towels next to each other, he added, "So he is your friend, I see."

As I sat on my towel, he towered above me, staring at me.

"Are you a moffie?" he asked.

"A what?" I responded

"A faggot? A queer?"

The word shocked me and frightened me. I had done nothing to upset this man, nor had I said anything to him that might cause him to say these things.

"Are you deaf? Are you a queer hanging around with a White guy?"

"He's my friend," I volunteered.

As I spoke, I felt a stinging sensation across my face and found myself sprawled on the sand, the man now kneeling next to me, hitting me. I cried out both in pain and in shock and felt another slap across my face. Sand was now flying up as we struggled – me to break free and him to attack me. Throughout his onslaught, he kept shouting, "Queer! Faggot! Fucking Black!"

As I lay on the sand, trying to protect my face I heard a loud shout.

"Hey! What's going on here?"

It was Peter. He rushed at the man and rugby tackled him, causing both of them to roll down the sand dune. Peter pinned him down and glared at the man.

"What the hell do you think you're doing?" shouted Peter.

"I suppose you're also a fucking queer like your Black friend there!"

Peter's eyes narrowed and I could see the anger in his face.

"Peter, leave him," I shouted. "Let him go."

Peter heard me and released his grip on the man, and then he stood up and told the man to 'beat it'. The man rose to his feet, cursing both Peter and me and sauntered down the sand dune, heading back to the Snake Park area.

"Are you OK, Raj?" asked Peter, comforting me by holding my face in his hands.

I suddenly burst into tears at the realisation of what had transpired. He pulled me close to him and I buried my face in his chest and sobbed. He gently stroked my hair, as my mother would do when my father attacked me in one of his drunken states, and tried to calm me down.

Once I managed to control my sobbing, I lifted my head and through tear-filled eyes I looked up at my saviour.

"Thank you for saving me, Peter."

He hugged me again and gently kissed the top of my head.

"Come; let's head back, away from this place."

We picked up our towels, dusted the sand from our bodies and put our clothes on, then headed back to where Peter had parked his motor bike. As we neared the area I suggested to Peter that we cut through the bushes to avoid the man, should he be lurking in the Snake Park area.

As we cut through the bushes, Peter stopped and turned to me.

"I'm truly sorry about what happened to you, Raj."

He wrapped his arms around me and kissed me gently on the lips, almost as though he didn't want to hurt them in case they were bruised or cut. As we cleared the bushes, Peter suggested that I stay where we were and he would fetch his motor bike and drive me to another bus stop, away from where the man might be.

Once Peter arrived back with his motor bike, I climbed on behind him and thought nothing if anyone saw a White and an Indian together on a bike. As I sat on the back of the motor bike, clutching tightly onto Peter's waist, I thought of the attack and tried to make sense of it. The words kept coming into my mind: "Queer! Moffie! Black!" I wondered if this was part of what was Apartheid. Why did this man use those words, when I had never heard Peter use them or Mr Walters, for that matter? When we reached a bus stop, Peter pulled over to the side of the road and stopped his bike so that I could alight. As I dismounted, I thanked Peter once again for coming to my assistance.

"Peter, what did that man mean by calling me a queer and a moffie and a Black?"

Peter seemed a little embarrassed before answering.

"I wouldn't take any notice of what he said, Raj. Forget about it. He's not worth worrying about. I'll give you a call during the week to see how you are, OK?"

"Thanks again, Peter."

Peter put his bike into gear and sped off, leaving me at the bus stop waiting for a bus. I didn't have to wait too long and was soon on my journey back into the centre of Durban and then heading back to Phoenix.

When I arrived home, earlier than expected, I didn't say anything about the beach incident to my mother.

It was fate that Aunty Selvie phoned our house that evening, because when she had spoken to my mother, I asked if I could talk to her on the phone. My mother left the lounge and when I knew that she was out of ear-shot, I asked Aunty Selvie to explain the words the man had used.

"When did this happen, my darling?" she asked.

"Today, at the beach," I whispered back over the phone so that no-one in our house would hear me.

"Raj, I'm not going to discuss this over the phone. Try to forget what was said, but when I see you next, I'll try to explain it all to you, but don't worry about it."

I thanked Aunty Selvie and knew in my heart that she would make all things right, and put down the phone.

CHAPTER 12

When I arrived home from school on Wednesday, I found Aunty Selvie sitting in our lounge, having tea and chatting to my mother. I was surprised to see her there because she seldom came to our house alone and during the day, so I wondered if something untoward had happened.

"Aunty Selvie's here to take you to her house for the evening for dinner, because she has some friends coming around who she wants you to meet," said my mother smiling broadly at me.

This seemed out of character both to be invited to meet friends and for my mother to be smiling so broadly, not that she ever smiled like that.

"What's the occasion?" I asked.

"Nothing in particular," replied Aunty Selvie. "It's just that I invited some friends around for dinner and I thought you might like to meet them. Uncle Harry has a meeting tonight, so he won't be there so I thought it would be good to have some friends around."

It still sounded odd to me. She didn't elaborate on who the friends might be, but being invited to Aunty Selvie's house was in itself an occasion that I would savour.

"I also thought you might like to bring a change of school clothes then if you want to stay the night at our house, I can take you to school in the morning," said Aunty Selvie.

"But it would be so far for you in the morning," I offered.

"It wouldn't be a problem and besides, I'd rather do that than have to bring you back home late at night."

"So run along my boy and get a bag packed," said my mother still beaming.

I wondered whether Aunty Selvie had said something to my mother about the 'words' I had asked her about and that perhaps they had been discussing me and my outing to the beach, but then I pushed that thought from my mind as I knew that whatever I said to Aunty Selvie in confidence, remained between us.

I packed a small bag with clean school clothes and changed into some casuals to wear to Aunty Selvie's, then the two of us set off to her house. On the way I asked her for more information about the planned evening, but she averted my discussion to focus on her own information gathering plan.

"Now, my darling, tell me everything that happened at the beach."

At first I was rather hesitant, but then I retold the events as they happened and spared nothing this time. I told her all about how I had arranged to go to the beach with Peter and how the man had approached me while I was waiting for Peter to arrive and how we had walked along the beach, our lying together in the sand dunes and Peter going for a swim. When I reached the part of the man attacking me in the sand dunes, I could feel a lump developing in my throat and thought I would burst into tears again as the scene became clear, once more, in my mind. Eventually, I was able to retell her exactly what had happened.

"My darling, you must understand that no matter what the events of the time are and no matter where you are there will always be people who say wicked things to others. So often these words, although they are hurtful, are said in spite or anger. Sometimes they are even said to antagonise one so that they provoke you to retaliate. There I am glad that you didn't do that, but you must be careful. This time it was fortunate that Peter was there to protect and save you from this man's ill behaviour, but there might be times when there will be no-one there to defend you, other than yourself."

I sat silently listening to her soft, calming voice, taking in every word she uttered.

"Raj, you must also understand that the fact that you have a male friend, whom you like very much, is not your fault, but you will find people who are prejudiced against such a relationship, and here I mean that they will pre-judge you, even though they do not understand your situation or the person for whom you have feelings."

"But why Aunty?"

"Often it is the way in which they are brought up by their families or society as a whole. You know how much emphasis we have in our own Indian community for a boy to get married and have a family, don't you?"

I nodded.

"Well, even in our society you might find some Indian men who will tease and antagonise you if they know that you like boys more than girls. It is not only the Whites who might do it to you as that man at the beach did, but it might even be your own kind. You must also understand that you have a double edged sword hanging over your head."

"What do you mean by that Aunty?"

"It's what I've spoken to you about before. In this country there is a great deal of antagonism towards men who like other men, on the one hand, and then you have the added disadvantage of liking a White boy. It's what I've told you, that in the Apartheid society we, who are looked at as being Black, shouldn't mix with Whites."

"But it was daylight and you had once said to me that Blacks and Whites meet during the day, but we have to be careful at night."

"Darling, it's not quite as simple as that. Sure, we do business together and that is usually conducted during the day, but once the sun sets, we must all go our separate ways; the Whites to the White's houses and the Indians to theirs."

I sat silently thinking as she drove along the highway on our way to her home.

"What would people think if I liked an Indian boy?"

My mind went to Morgan and wondered if this was acceptable in our society.

"It would probably be very similar, the only difference being that you wouldn't be intimidated by White men, but I can assure you that the Indian men would be no different. It is best if you keep your secrets to yourself and those very close to you whom you can trust. Let me tell you a little about tonight. I have invited some of my close friends who understand about issues like yours, so that you can talk to them if you'd like to, to discuss your feelings with them."

"Are they your Indian friends?"

"And Mr Walters will be there."

Hearing that made me a little happier as I liked Mr Walters and felt I could talk openly with him, much like I did with Aunty Selvie.

When we arrived at Aunty Selvie's house, she showed me to my room so I unpacked my bag and then I went into the kitchen where she was busy getting the dinner preparations organised.

At 7:00 that evening, Mr Walters was the first to arrive with two friends.

"Hi Raj. Nice to see you again. How are you?"

"Hello Mr Walters. I'm fine thanks, and you?"

"I'm well, but let me introduce you to my friends here. Raj, this is Michael, and Vanesh. Guys, this is Raj."

We all politely shook hands and although they were older than me, they were not as old as Aunty Selvie or Mr Walters.

"Michael is an interior decorator who helped with the décor of your aunty's house, and Vanesh is an art teacher."

"I think you did a very good job, Michael," I said, smiling enigmatically at him.

"Thanks, Raj, but I did very little; it was your aunty who did most of the work."

Michael looked no more than early thirty, was well dressed and White, like Mr Walters, and Vanesh was probably in his late twenty's and Indian.

Soon the doorbell was ringing again and more visitors arrived. This time there were three young Indian men who looked to be between the ages of twenty-four and thirty. Mr Walters, Michael and Vanesh welcomed them each by hugging them, while I shook their hands when I was introduced to them. Aunty Selvie, in the meantime was busy pouring drinks for everyone who wanted something to drink. I also noticed how well-dressed and well-groomed these three young men were. At approximately 7:30, dinner was ready so we all sat down to eat. Aunty Selvie had placed me between herself and one of the young Indian men by the name of Brian. Across from me sat Michael and Vanesh, while Mr Walters and the other two Indian men sat next to Aunty Selvie.

The delicious smelling curry, along with the condiments, was placed on the table for us to help ourselves. The company was chatty and easy-going, and everyone was soon tucking into this heart-warming meal, complimenting Aunty Selvie's meal. For those who wanted it, wine was supplied, but I comforted myself with my glass of lemonade. I listened as the conversations changed from current political topics to art and then to literature.

"You know I spoke to you, Raj, earlier about certain aspects of the Apartheid regime," said Aunty Selvie, "well, when I was studying, we were also monitored as to what we could and could not read."

"You mean books?" I enquired.

"Yes, my darling. The government decided what we could and could not see or read. There are men who are basically self-styled moralists who make judgements about what constitutes acceptable literature and what doesn't. In this country we have police who look at crime such as murder and robbery, and then we have people who look out to see what we are reading and looking at. I suppose you could call them the literature or film police, if you so wished."

"How did you study?"

"We were limited as to what books we could get access to and so in some parts, you could say our education was limiting. However, there were some people who made it their duty to try to get what was classified as banned literature, just to get a balanced point of view about worldly issues, just as there are still people today who are defying the bans on literature."

I was shocked to hear that the government dictated what we could read and what films we could see. I had thought we had free access to whatever we wanted to see and read, but this was obviously not the case.

Michael broached the topic of theatre and then my ears pricked up. I still remembered the night that Uncle Harry and Aunty Selvie had taken me to the theatre at the university; the night I first spoke to Morgan.

"I've been asked to design the set for an upcoming production that Natal University drama students are doing, so I've asked Vanesh to help me," said Michael beaming at Vanesh as he said it.

Apart from a possible artistic link, I saw no other link connecting these two men, but somehow they seemed to enjoy each other's company and smiled a great deal at each other.

"What show is that, Michael?" enquired Aunty Selvie.

"The Importance of Being Earnest," answered Michael.

"Oh, that should be fun," said Aunty Selvie, excitedly. "When are they doing it?"

"It's going to be after the July holidays. Do you want me to get tickets for you?"

"That would be wonderful, Michael, but could I ask you a favour please?"

"Sure, anything."

"Could I have four tickets please? Two for Harry and me and one for Raj."

I looked surprised at Aunty Selvie.

"But that's only three of us," I commented.

"Yes, I know, but I'm sure that you'd like to bring a friend along, wouldn't you?"

I was flabbergasted and didn't know what to say; in fact I was suddenly silent.

"You look shocked, Raj," said Aunty Selvie, smiling gleefully at me. "I'm sure that you have a friend that you would like to accompany you, haven't you?"

I stammered while everyone around the table looked at me, waiting to hear my answer.

"Thank you Aunty Selvie and thank you Michael," I managed to get out.

"Do you have a friend?" enquired Mr Walters.

I threw a glance at Aunty Selvie as if to say 'Help!' I didn't know whether I should say anything about Peter or Morgan for that matter.

"I'm sure that my good-looking nephew has many friends, don't you?"

I could feel myself blush, and took a gulp of my cold drink.

"Why don't you ask Peter," she continued.

I nearly choked on my cold drink as she said Peter's name. I felt that I had been exposed to the world. I almost felt as though I had been betrayed. How could she say Peter's name in front of these strangers?

"I believe Peter is a very nice young man who might enjoy an evening out at the theatre," said Aunty Selvie, stretching an arm to take hold of my hand, to comfort me.

I felt a gentle squeeze as she held my hand in hers. It was a comforting sensation and any anger or concern I might have had because of her mentioning Peter's name, disappeared.

"Peter saved Raj's life recently," said Aunty Selvie proudly.

"Why what happened?" enquired Brian.

Before I could say anything, Aunty Selvie once again took control of the situation.

"First I must tell you that Peter seems a very nice young White boy that Raj has befriended. Raj was recently at the beach with Peter when one of these oafs, that's the only word I can think of, came up to Raj and began intimidating him while Peter was swimming in the sea, then he hit Raj. Fortunately Peter arrived in the nick of time to save Raj from further assault and they sent this man on his way."

"Was it a White man?" asked Mr Walters.

"Oh yes," replied Aunty Selvie, "the kind of person who is obsessed with violence and seems also to have a problem with his sexuality. He called Raj a queer and a moffie and wanted to know if Peter was his boyfriend – that type of person."

By this time I was cringing with embarrassment. The whole table was hearing about my romantic attachment to Peter and how I was beaten up on the beach.

"You say Peter is a White boy?" asked Michael, empathy emanating through his voice.

I made eye-contact with him and nodded.

"Raj, you mustn't feel bad. If you feel strongly about Peter, then that's a good sign," continued Michael.

"Not in this country," interrupted Mr Walters.

"What I mean is that you mustn't worry about him being White and you being Indian. If you like someone or love them, colour shouldn't come into the equation. It shouldn't be an issue. Sure, it's hard to maintain a relationship like that in this country, but if you mean so much to each other, you'll find a way to overcome anything; not so Vanesh?"

Vanesh took hold of Michael's hand and the two of them grinned at each other.

Again I looked surprised.

"Are you two…?"

"Yes Raj, Vanesh and I have been together now for close on a year and we're very happy together. There have been problems both from his family and mine, but because we feel so strongly for each other, we've tried to overcome those issues."

"Have you been abused at all?" I tentatively asked.

"Regularly," replied Vanesh. "When I was at art school I realised that I was gay and it was at a party like this that I met Michael and we started going out. At first we were very discreet because of the racial problems, but we found that there were many others in society who were also suffering as much as we were, being discriminated against, but we noticed it was mainly the adults who caused unhappiness for us. The people who were our ages seemed to accept us without questioning."

"And do you live together?"

"Yes," answered Michael. "At first it was difficult and we would sneak around in the dark to be with each other, but then we decided that we had nothing to hide and Vanesh moved in with me because his family felt that their family name had been defiled."

I then turned to Brian and the other two Indian men and looked at them as if to ask if they were party to Michael and Vanesh's 'secret'.

Aunty Selvie noticed my looking at the men and the expression on my face.

"Raj, with the exception of Mr Walters, all the men here tonight are gay," said Aunty Selvie. "I invited them so that you could meet other people like yourself and to know that although you might think that you are alone in the world with your problems, in fact you are not. I'm also sure that any one of them will tell you that they have gone through similar instances like you went through on the beach, where they have been called names, beaten up, intimidated and shamed simply because they have either the wrong colour skin or liked the wrong sort of person. If you can learn to overcome the intimidation, you will grow into a very strong person; someone who will be able to mature and integrate well in this land of ours."

One of the two Indian men, who had said very little all night, spoke up.

"Raj," he said, pointing to his accompanying friend, "Sanjeev and I have been together just on six months and neither of our families accepts us, but we are so happy together."

"Why don't they accept you?" I queried.

"To them it's an insult to the family name to be gay. They feel they would not only lose face within their communities, but we wouldn't be having grandchildren for them to boast about, so we've moved out of our families' homes and moved in together. It seems that our parents are only concerned about their positions in society and worry about themselves, rather than accepting that their children might be different from them and want to lead a different lifestyle. Obviously there are times when we miss our families, but this is our choice and we're happy with it. If others can't show some respect for the fact that we love each other, then we don't need those types of people in our lives. We've moved into the centre of Durban away from the Indian communities and we're happy where we are."

I sat transfixed, listening to these stories, realising why Aunty Selvie had arranged this dinner – to open my eyes to what was happening to people around me.

"I hear all your stories, but there are two things that concern me," I said, with an air of uncertainty. "The first is that it concerns me how you should have to leave your homes and families because of the person that you like. I have heard the saying that 'blood is thicker than water', but I am ashamed to think that my own flesh and blood would want to disown me because I like another boy and not a girl. Surely my love for my mother and father wouldn't diminish just because I fell in love with a boy?"

The group sat transfixed by my statement.

"And second, you are all adults and I'm still at school – a child. I can't leave home like you might have and there is no way that I and my friend can move in together, so how am I going to benefit from your advice?"

Aunty Selvie laughed. "My darling, no one expects you to do any of those things. The reason that I invited my friends around tonight was so that firstly, you could meet new people who might be in positions to help and advise you later on in life and secondly, to show you that you are not alone in this world and that the problems that you are encountering are universal. All of them have gone through what you are going through in various ways. Sanjeev and Krish have had to contend with Indian discrimination because their families believe that their family names have been disgraced; Michael and Vanesh have had to contend not only with their families feeling hurt by their love, but they have had to contend with the government's rulings as well. Many years ago Mr Walters and I went through the same situation, but fortunately we have remained friends ever since. My point is that whatever choices you make in life, they are your choices and you shouldn't let others stand in the way of your choices. Don't let other people make you feel guilty because of what you believe in; believe in yourself and make your choices wisely."

"Hear, hear," retorted Mr Walters, raising his glass of wine in a toast.

Aunty Selvie excused herself from the table and went off to the kitchen, soon to return with a plate of sweetmeats, which she placed in the centre of the table. The plate was an exotic, colourful, array of food. Everyone gasped in awe at the sight.

"I'm glad to hear all your responses to my sweetmeats, but Raj I want you to take particular notice of them."

"They look absolutely delicious Aunty Selvie."

"Before you tuck into them, Raj, I want you to look carefully at them. Notice that each one is a different colour from the others and each will have a different texture to it as well as a different flavour. Look at them as you might look at people. In our country we have many different colours and within each one of us, we are different, but, just as the plate looks enticing to you, so we should look at ourselves in our society in the same way. Each of us is different, yet together we make an enticing array of people who each has so much to offer. Just as there might be some on the plate that you don't like that much, so there are people who we don't like sometimes, and just as there will be sweetmeats that we can't get enough of, so there will be people in our lives that we feel the same way about. Now, as you take each one to taste, treat your friends in the same way and realise that the choices for taking a particular cake or sweet will be similar to the reasons why you have chosen to befriend a particular person or not."

I smiled at her as she spoke, tears beginning to well-up in my eyes.

"You are so wise Aunty Selvie. Thank you, and thank you for bringing your friends into my life. Tonight has made such a difference in my life already," I replied, wiping a tear from my eyes.

I really felt differently, possibly because things were coming out into the open and I had met others who were in a similar situation to me and this made a big difference to me.

Our conversations shifted from me to them and back to me and school and how I could deal with situations that might arise in the school environment, but one thing still bothered me.

"Aunty Selvie, there is one thing I want to ask you. Does my mother know about me and Peter?"

"Not unless you have told her," was her quick reply.

"It's just that when you were at our house, she seemed so different towards me when you told me I was coming here tonight."

"My darling, I think it was more a case of you being away from your father than her knowing about you. She loves you, no matter what your feelings might be about other people, but about your liking of boys – I certainly haven't told her anything."

"And Uncle Harry, does he know?"

"No, but even if he did, he wouldn't say anything to your family. Your secret is safe with me."

This was why I liked Aunty Selvie the best of all my uncles and aunts; she told things as they were and I could trust her.

The evening soon came to a close with the arrival of Uncle Harry. He greeted everyone and joined us in the lounge while we had coffee together and chattered casually to Mr Walters. Uncle Harry seemed very much at ease with his guests and when they all left, kissing each other, it didn't seem to bother Uncle Harry when Michael and Vanesh kissed the others goodbye.

After everyone left, I helped Aunty Selvie tidy up before going to bed. I didn't fall asleep immediately as my mind was a rush of thoughts. Tonight had been an eye-opener to me and I was so grateful to Aunty Selvie for what she had done for me.

I was up bright and early the next morning, ready for school and with a new outlook on life, a new attitude and a will to challenge anyone.

When Aunty Selvie dropped me off at school, as she promised she would do, I kissed her gently on the cheek and repeated my 'thank you' from the previous evening. She really was a wonderful woman.

CHAPTER 13

Peter had phoned as he had promised and I told him very briefly of my dinner at Aunty Selvie's house, but didn't elaborate on what was discussed or who the other guests were, as I said I would tell him all about our discussions when he returned from his rugby tour to the Cape. However, I did tell Sarisha everything about the dinner party.

"How I would have loved to have been there to hear your aunt's wisdom, Raj. And the men; were they nice?"

"They were very friendly towards me," I replied.

"Yes, but were they nice. You know what I mean!"

"You mean did I find them attractive?"

"Of course. What else did you think I meant?"

"Yes they were all very good looking," I coyly replied.

"Did you make a date with any of them?" continued Sarisha with her interrogation.

"Of course not," I sharply retorted. "They were in relationships together. But my aunt is going to get tickets for a show from Michael. He's a larney interior decorator."

"Is he handsome?" asked Sarisha, snuggling up closer to me as if to keep our conversation secret.

"Very, but he's got a boyfriend called Vanesh who's an art teacher."

"Is Michael, White or Indian?"

"White but Vanesh is Indian."

"Idiot! I know that. I wouldn't think some White mother would call her son Vanesh! And are you going to see them again?"

"I don't know. They're much older than me and I don't have their addresses or phone numbers, so I probably won't see them again."

"You fool! Why didn't you at least get their phone numbers?"

"I didn't think of it."

"Did Morgan's name come up at all during your conversations?"

I hadn't really thought of Morgan during the dinner. My thoughts had been on Peter and Aunty Selvie's guests.

"No, actually it didn't," I answered, "but tell me, have you seen Alvin at all?" changing the subject.

"Don't talk to me about him," retorted Sarisha, angrily.

"Why not? I thought you were having some sort of relationship with him?"

"He only wants one thing. Morgan was right you know."

"And what's that one thing?" I taunted.

"Don't be stupid, Raj. You know what that is – sex."

"And you don't want to oblige," I sniggered.

"Would you?"

"Not with him, thanks very much; but if you're serious about dropping him, I'm glad because I didn't really like him and nor did Morgan, and in any case, I think you deserve someone better than that."

"Why thanks Raj. That's very kind of you to say so. However, why didn't you say something to me earlier?"

I laughed at her question.

"Because you wouldn't have listened to me, and you certainly didn't want to listen to Morgan the night of the party."

"I just thought he was saying things to me because he was jealous," replied Sarisha, rather embarrassedly. "Now tell me, what is this show you're supposed to be getting tickets for?"

"It's a play that the University students are putting on; it's called 'The Importance of Being Earnest', and Michael is designing the set for them, so he can get tickets."

"Ooh, I love that play. It's so funny," replied Sarisha.

"Would you like to come with me when I get the tickets?"

"What about Peter. Didn't you want to take him along with you?"

I hesitated, not because she had mentioned Peter's name, but I wasn't sure whether Whites and Indians would be allowed to be at the same venue together and at night. What would the police or the government say and do? After all, when I went to the theatre with Aunty Selvie, there had been no Whites there.

"I don't know if I'd be allowed to invite him," I answered.

"Why ever not?"

"You know! Apartheid!"

"Oh, I see what you mean. Why don't you check with your aunt and if you are allowed to take him, then do so, but if not, then I'd love to go."

"Are you doing anything in particular over these holidays, Sarisha?"

"No, nothing special. Why, did you have something in mind?"

"Not really. I just thought we might meet up with Morgan and do something, or go to movies, perhaps."

"Certainly not to see Tarzan going to India again," said Sarisha, with a glint in her eye.

"I'm sure he would have reached India by now," I laughed. "No, but think about it."

We said our goodbyes and she returned to her home while I stayed and played with my little brothers, something that they enjoyed and that I found tiresome sometimes, but it was holidays and they loved it when I was at home with them.

Two days later, the phone at home rang and my mother called to say that there was someone on the line for me.

"Who is it Amah?" I enquired before answering the phone.

"I don't know I didn't ask, but it sounds like a young man."

I took the phone from her and waited until she was out of earshot before starting to speak.

"Hello, Raj here," I whispered.

"Hi buddy. Why are you whispering," replied the voice.

"Is that you Morgan?"

"Who did you think it was?"

I wasn't sure whether it was Peter phoning from Cape Town, and even though it wasn't, it was nice to hear Morgan's voice.

"Sorry, but I didn't know who it might be. How are you?"

"I'm well, and yourself?"

"Not too bad, just being driven slightly mad by my two smaller brothers who pester me to play with them all the time."

"Well, how would you like to have a break from them for a while?"

"Why, what did you have in mind?"

"My cousin in Pietermariztburg asked if I wanted to go and spend some time with their family during the holidays and I wondered if you'd like to come with me."

"That sounds like fun, but I'd better ask my mother," I answered, knowing that Amah wouldn't object. "But who else will be there?"

"It's just you and me going. My older brother will drive us there and fetch us at the end of the week, but I just thought it might be nice to get away from here for a while."

"Morgan, can I speak to my mother and then get back to you?"

"No problem, but if possible can you let me know by tonight at the latest."

"You don't have to worry because I'll get back to you within an hour at the latest."

"Great. Looking forward to hearing from you. Cheers, Raj."

I replaced the phone and went into the kitchen where my mother was busy preparing lunch for us children.

"Amah, that was a school friend of mine and he wants to know if I'd like to go to Pietermaritzburg with him for a week. Can I please go?"

"Where will you be staying?"

"With his cousin's family," I answered.

"I'm sure it will be fine. I'll tell your father, but I'm sure that he won't object."

"Thanks, Amah," I replied, kissing her on the cheek and running back to make the phone call through to Morgan.

I stood waiting, listening to the phone ringing on the other end. Eventually the phone was answered and I recognised Morgan's voice.

"Morgan! It's me," I called out excitedly. "My mother said it would be fine for me to go with you. When are we going?"

"Tomorrow morning. We can pick you up at your place at around 9:00am, if that's OK with you?"

"That sounds great. Oh, and must I bring anything with me?"

"Clothes, swimming costume and some money, that's all."

"Great. I'll see you tomorrow then. Cheers."

I replaced the phone and stood smiling to myself. What a pleasure to have a week away from Durban and the family. A week with Morgan! I wondered how Sarisha might feel if she knew that I was going away with Morgan, so I decided not to tell her, just in case she tried to kill me out of jealousy!

The following morning, true to his word, Morgan and his brother arrived at our house. I heard the car's hooter tooting outside and so I rushed to the front door, waved and shouted that I was almost ready. My mother came out to greet the two young men in the car and to make sure that I was actually going with them to Pietermaritzburg, not that she didn't trust me, but mothers are like that; they like to make doubly sure of their children's behaviour.

"You take good care of my son," I heard my mother telling Morgan and his brother.

"You don't have to worry about a thing. He'll be well looked after, I can promise you," replied Morgan.

I rushed from the house with my suitcase, kissed my mother goodbye, threw my bag into the boot of the car and climbed into the back seat. The engine roared and off we set, Morgan and I waving to my mother and baby brothers.

Morgan introduced me to his older brother, Clinton, who looked like a smaller, yet older version of Morgan, and the three of us were soon deep in conversation about the trip and our stay in Pietermaritzburg.

"I've always heard that Pietermaritzburg is such a dump," I said as we headed inland.

"It can be, but on the other hand, you can have great fun there," answered Morgan.

"That depends if you have a girlfriend to keep you company," replied Clinton.

I wasn't quite sure how to take that statement, but chose not to respond; instead Morgan turned to me in the back seat and winked.

"You must excuse my brother. All he ever thinks about is girls, girls, and girls. I sometimes wonder if he ever has any other interests in life other than girls!"

"But seriously, Morgan, what does one do in Pietermaritzburg?"

"We can go to the pub and swim in my cousin's swimming pool and…" said Morgan.

He hesitated for some time as though in some suspended animation.

"Yes… and? And what?" I asked.

Clinton burst out laughing.

"You see what I mean about having a girl with you! There's nothing else to do. That's why they call this place 'Sleepy Hollow'.

Morgan looked somewhat embarrassed by his brother's quip, but rapidly added, "At least we've got each other's company, and so I don't think we'll get too bored."

Driving to Pietermaritzburg didn't take long and we were soon heading up past Mountain Rise cemetery on our way to Morgan's cousin's house in the suburb of Northdale.

The house, when we reached it, looked very ordinary from the outside, but when we entered, I could see that the family had decorated it with an element of class, without it being overdone. I was introduced to his cousin, Neelan, who was about our ages, tall and slim. To me, Neelan looked the sporty type, much like Morgan and I presumed that perhaps that's why they got on so well. I must confess that I didn't really get on with any of my cousins I might have, no matter how many times removed!

Neelan's parents were not home as they were both working, but his mother would be home later in the day as she was a nursing sister at Northdale Hospital and would be going off shift. His father apparently was an accountant for a firm in the centre of Pietermaritzburg and so he'd only be home in the early evening.

Neelan offered us something to drink and then showed Morgan and me to our room. We would be sharing, which suited me, as I would be able to lie in bed and chat to Morgan, something I couldn't really do with my younger brothers. We unpacked our suitcases and put our clothes away, and then we went out into the garden next to the swimming pool. Clinton, in the meantime, had decided to make the return journey to Durban, probably so that he could spend more time with his girlfriend.

"You have a beautiful home here, Neelan," I said, wandering around the garden with its profusion of azaleas all in bloom.

"Thanks, Raj. It is quite attractive at this time of the year. But listen guys; don't you want to take a swim?"

"I'm all for it, but isn't the water cold?" asked Morgan.

"Surprisingly no," replied Neelan, "maybe because it's not a large area of water to heat up from the sun."

"Come on Raj, let's get into our costumes."

The two of us hurried back to our room and stripped off. I pulled on my swimming shorts, but watched out of the corner of my eye, as Morgan slid his lithe body into a black Speedo. He looked so attractive bare-chested in his Speedo. He caught me watching him and he smiled but never said or did anything. He picked up his towel and headed out to the pool with me following closely behind. As soon as we appeared in the garden, so Neelan headed indoors to put on his costume. Soon the three of us were frolicking in the refreshingly cool water. We swam, splashed and dive-bombed each other and then lay out on our towels allowing the warm sun to dry us. As we lay there in the sun, I glanced at Neelan and saw that he too had a defined athletic body, much like Morgan's and he too had on a Speedo in bright yellow, which contrasted against the dark colour of his smooth skin.

After spending about an hour at the pool, Neelan suggested that we go in and have something to eat and maybe play some video games, which we did. By approximately four in the afternoon, Neelan's mother returned home from work and I was introduced to her. She seemed a very charming lady who insisted that I call her Claudia. She chatted with both Morgan and me, asking how school was and how Morgan's parents were, and then at about 5:30pm, Neelan's father returned home. He was a short, rotund man, completely the opposite in physique to Neelan, but just as friendly and cheerful as his wife and son.

"How do you do, Mr Govender," I said, shaking hands with him.

"And are you a friend of Morgan's?" he asked.

I thought this rather an odd question as I had accompanied Morgan to Neelan's house, so one would presume that we were friends.

"We're at the same school, uncle," answered Morgan.

"Oh, and do you like cricket like Morgan does, Raj?"

"I like to watch, Mr Govender, but I find playing the game boring. To stand out in the sun all day often not even getting near the ball to me is a waste of time."

"But you're happy to watch this boring game?"

I couldn't let on that it was more the players that I enjoyed watching and not so much the actual game.

"Yes, sir," I sheepishly replied.

"Well, never mind. There are times when I feel the same way about the game. It can be a long, drawn-out affair to which there is no result and for five days you've endured this pain of watching." He shook his head. "I like the limited over games. They're much more exciting to watch."

"I agree," I responded, smiling at him to show that perhaps we had something in common – the dislike for wasting valuable time.

That evening, after a sumptuous dinner, while Neelan's parents sat in the lounge listening to the radio, the three of us went into the games room, which they had, and played games. After spending something like two hours of games, Neelan suggested we go for a drink.

"Where are we going?" I enquired of Neelan.

"We'll nip into the hotel. It's just up the road from here, so we can walk if you like."

"But aren't we under age?" was my question.

Both Morgan and Neelan looked at me and both had wry smiles on their faces.

"No!" replied Morgan, emphatically.

"But I'm not eighteen yet," I continued.

"Raj, you don't have to worry about a thing, provided you don't advertise the fact that you're under age."

"But what if we get caught drinking in the bar and being under age?"

"A very good friend of the family runs the hotel and we sneak in where they've got a snooker table and have our drinks there. So are we going?"

I felt a little awkward about being under age in a hotel bar, but both Morgan and Neelan kept reassuring me that all would be well.

Neelan told his parents where we were going and they seemed quite at ease with the knowledge that we were going to the hotel, so off we set.

At the hotel, Neelan led us through the foyer, down a long corridor and into a fairly large room with a snooker table in its centre and a bar counter to one side. Around the walls of the room were scattered small tables and chairs, while at the bar counter were a number of high bar stools. The room wasn't crowded, but at the bar sat about four adults, while at the snooker table were two young men having a game.

"Do you mind if we have a game after you?" asked Neelan of one of the players, who gladly agreed.

"What do you want to drink, Raj?" asked Morgan.

I didn't know what to say. I had drunk beers before, but in private. Here we were in the public eye and I kept thinking about the under age element.

"A coke will be fine thanks Morgan," I replied.

"Come on have something a little stronger than that," came his response.

"OK. A beer then," I whispered, hoping that no-one would hear me.

"Neelan, what are you going to have?" asked Morgan.

"Beer for me too, please."

Morgan gave the barman our order and I watched as he eyed us. I was worrying that he might ask for some type of identification to prove that we were over the legal age, but he never did. Instead Morgan arrived at the table where we were sitting carrying three beers.

"Cheers," said Morgan, heartily. "Here's to us."

"To us and our holiday," echoed Neelan.

"To us," I whispered, again hoping that no-one overheard me.

The cold flavoursome beer slid down my throat making me feel warm inside. It had a smooth taste that I knew would make me want more, but I also knew that I couldn't get out of control and get drunk.

The first beer went down smoothly and so did the second. By the time we got to our third, the snooker table was available for us to have a game. Because there were three of us, we asked one of the young guys who had been playing if he wanted to partner one of us so we had two teams of two each. Morgan chose me to partner him and Neelan took the young man whose name was Ronnie.

I had never actually played a game of snooker, but I had seen others playing it so I had a fair idea of what to do, but I think it was beginners luck for me as we began the game. Morgan was surprised at the skill I showed in potting a number of red balls.

"Hey, you look as though you've played this game all your life," he joked as I sank another ball.

"Beginner's luck," I chirped, the beer making me feel more relaxed.

We continued on our winning ways and eventually Morgan and I ran out winners. For my outrageously successful play, Morgan instinctively gave me a victory hug. I wasn't sure how to respond to this public affection, but I enjoyed his close presence and allowed him to squeeze my body against his. More drinks flowed as a result of our win, and a revenge game was decided upon. This time Neelan and his partner, Ronnie managed to wipe us off the table so to speak.

"One all!" shouted Morgan. "We have to have a play-off."

"Agreed!" replied Neelan.

By this time my head was beginning to spin ever so slightly and when I tried to focus on the balls, I wasn't quite sure whether I was seeing one or two at a time.

"I hope I'm not going to let you down," I whispered to Morgan. "I think I've had too much to drink."

"Don't worry, we'll make the most of it and beat these guys. You can do it, I know you can."

My aim was beginning to go astray and I was missing a few shots and at one stage, Morgan stood right up behind me as he tried to hold the cue steady as I lined up a shot. Feeling his warm body pressed up tightly against mine could have distracted me, but fortunately, I never miss-cued my shot and he managed to sink a ball when it came to his turn. The game swung back and forth until we were left with the black ball on the table and Neelan to take a shot at it. He aimed and missed.

"Two shots for us!" shouted Morgan, whose turn it was.

He gently stroked the white ball allowing it to tap the black ball in the direction of one of the side pockets, and then with ease he tapped the white ball so that it nudged the black ball into the pocket. We had won. Should I rather say Morgan had won because I didn't really contribute to that win. He yelped with glee and jumped into the air, then hugged me again profusely. I thought if he hugged me any harder, all the beer that I had consumed that evening would come rushing up and embarrass both of us. We thanked our opponents for the games and then decided that I had drunk enough, so it was time to head home.

Back home, Morgan and I said goodnight to Neelan and stumbled our way to our room, trying as best as possible not to wake Neelan's parents who had already gone to bed.

"You're quite a player," said Morgan as he pulled off his shirt.

"I'm sorry if I let you down in any way in our game, Morgan, but the more beers I drank the more difficult it became for me to see the balls properly."

He chuckled.

"Hey, I think for a first timer, you did very well. Now let's get into bed and go to sleep."

I kicked off my shoes and then took off my shirt and undid my jeans I was wearing. I fell onto my bed in my effort to get my legs free from my jeans and as I did so I began giggling.

"Sh! You'll wake the family, Raj."

"Sorry!" I hissed.

I sat on the edge of my bed in my white underpants watching as Morgan removed his jeans, effortlessly. He folded his jeans and placed then on the chest of drawers then returned to his bed, pulled down the blankets and slipped under the sheets.

"Must I put the light out?" I asked, slurring my words.

"Oh sorry Raj, would you mind?"

"Not at all."

I rose from my bed and staggered to the light switch by the door. I closed our bedroom door, switched off the light and began to fumble my way back to my bed in the dark. I slammed into the foot of my bed.

"Ow! Shit!" I exclaimed, as I rubbed my shin.

"Are you alright?" asked Morgan.

"I'll survive, but I can't see a thing. Just talk quietly to me so I know where you are then I can find my way to my bed."

"I'm over here," whispered Morgan. "I think you played exceptionally well tonight and I think that between the two of us we could whip the pants off anyone who wanted to play snooker against us."

I reached my bed and thanked Morgan for talking in an effort to guide me to the bed.

"Goodnight Morgan, sleep well."

"You too, Raj."

Silence fell … then out of the silence came a long, low fart.

"Sorry," whispered Morgan.

CHAPTER 14

Our days spent in Pietermaritzburg were far from boring and I realised, much like Morgan did, that one didn't need to have a girlfriend to have fun. We went shopping with Claudia to buy groceries and one evening, Mr Govender took us all to movies. Although Pietermaritzburg was very similar to Durban, except for the sea, we spent most of our time among the Indian community. The only way I can describe the people of Northdale is to say they were 'provincial'. They seemed more laid-back than the people of Durban and in some ways life resembled something in slow motion.

We had been to the hotel a couple of times and on each visit Morgan and I had beaten Neelan and whatever partner he could find at snooker. With each game Morgan became more impressed with my play and even suggested that I had visited bars in Durban to play snooker or I'd had lessons. I was glad that there was something that I could do equally as well as Morgan, because I looked up to him as being a talented sportsman and me a mere nerd.

One day, Neelan had to go to visit a friend of his mother's to collect something from her. So Morgan and I remained at the house lounging next to the pool. The day was an exceptionally hot sunny day so swimming was the order of the day. We lay next to each other absorbing the sun's rays and then jumping into the refreshing water to cool down.

"Morgan, do you have a girlfriend?" I asked as we lay letting the sun dry us after a swim.

"No. And you?"

I shook my head.

"The only female friend I have is Sarisha."

"Why did you ask?"

"I just wondered. Seeing that your brother went on so much about girls I thought maybe you followed in his footsteps."

"I leave that to him. I've got other things that interest me, so I don't have much time for girls."

"Things like what?" I enquired.

"Oh, sport and things."

Silence fell on the conversation for a while.

"Morgan, do your parents put pressure on you to get a girlfriend?"

"Sometimes they do, but I tend to brush it aside. I think my Dad puts more pressure on me than my Mum. What about you?"

"My parents don't really say anything to me, but I think my Dad probably says things behind my back."

"And your Mum; what does she say?"

"Nothing much. She has said on occasions how nice it would be for her to be a granny, but I think that's all they worry about, being grandparents."

"Do you ever think you'll get married?" queried Morgan.

I turned to face him and stared long and hard into his eyes as he waited for my answer.

"No, Morgan. I suppose I'm too young to think of things like that."

It was a short, to-the-point answer, but I felt it gave Morgan the answer he might have been searching for. I hadn't said I was gay, but I hoped that he could read between the lines, so to speak. He smiled briefly, rose from his prone position and dived into the swimming pool. I lay there watching him swim a couple of lengths until he came to rest at the deep end of the pool.

"What about you?" I shouted to him.

"I don't know. Maybe one day I might get married, but at the moment, I haven't given it any thought."

This answer flooded my mind and I was now beginning to get mixed messages from Morgan. Had I presumed too much about him or had I merely fantasized what I would have liked to have thought, but then my mind raced back to our outing at the movies to see Tarzan going to India and where his leg had rested erotically against mine.

"Do you think you would be pressured into marrying?" I asked.

"I don't know. People close to you can really be persuasive some times and sometimes you do things just to keep others happy, so who knows."

"I wouldn't let anyone pressure me into doing something that I knew would make me unhappy; would you?"

He remained silent for a while, obviously thinking about what I had asked.

"It's hard sometimes to ignore what your parents, for example, want."

"But Morgan, you're an individual with a mind of your own. Surely you can make your own decisions."

"Raj, sometimes it's not that easy. You get pressure not only from your family but also from the community in which you live, not to mention the government."

My ears pricked up when he mentioned the word 'government'.

"How does the government put pressure on you?"

"I suppose it's in ways that you can't mix with whomever you like. I would like to go where I want and mix with anyone I want. I don't want to be told what to do."

"But that tends to contradict what you said earlier."

"What do you mean?"

"You said that it was hard to ignore what your parents want from you; they're telling you what to do!"

"But that's different."

"How's it different? By doing what others want, and it's usually for their own good, makes you lose your individuality. Be yourself. Be true to who you are and not be something false that society has made you."

"Raj, where does all this philosophical talk come from?"

I laughed.

"Probably from my aunt, I suppose."

"Why from her?"

"I have this aunty, Selvie, who's very wise, in my opinion, and recently I spent a night at her house and I had my eyes opened to who I am."

"And who are you?"

I smiled at Morgan's concerned look on his face.

"You'll learn about me in time, but until then, I'll probably remain an enigma to you."

He climbed from the pool, his wet Speedo clinging to his body and outlining his thick appendage and came and lay on his towel next to me.

"You know I like you very much, Raj. I think that you make a good friend."

"Thanks for the compliment, Morgan; and I like you equally, but I see you as more than a good friend."

Morgan stretched and his hand glanced across my shoulder. It was like an electric shock reverberating through my body as he touched me. I smiled at the slight gesture and he noticed my smile.

"What are you smiling at?"

"You. You're a very sweet person, but don't be afraid of showing your feelings; it's all part of your individuality."

I rested my hand next to his shoulder and let my fingers touch his skin ever so gently; so gently in fact that he might have thought it was the wind breezing over him. He never moved away from my touch. My fingers moved a little more firmly against his shoulder and soon I wrapped my hand around his bicep. He glanced at me, his eyes piercing into mine, but without anger or malice.

"You've got big muscles," I said, almost breaking the tension around us.

He laughed at my comment but let me feel his muscles. He never rejected my touch; instead, he flexed his arms so that his biceps bulged.

"What about those?" he joked, as he tensed his arms.

"Those look really good. I feel well and truly protected with those arms near me."

He relaxed his arms and let the arm that I had held rest against my side. I felt his fingers moving in search of mine until we clasped each other's hand. Our fingers became entwined and our grip on each other's hand became firm as we squeezed.

Our eyes met and he smiled once more.

"I really do like you Raj," he said sliding his body closer to mine while still remaining attached to my hand.

I closed my eyes and enjoyed the moment, but this moment was soon shattered by the loud greetings from Neelan, who had arrived home. Both our hands flew apart hoping that Neelan hadn't seen us holding hands.

"Hi cuz, how's your day been?" asked Morgan.

"Have you two been here at the pool ever since I left you this morning?"

"Yep. We've been swimming, talking, tanning and generally being laid-back," continued Morgan.

"Well I'm glad you two managed to get some rest because tonight we're going to a farewell party."

"Great, where?" asked Morgan.

"As this is going to be your last night here, some friends have invited us to their place and my Dad has agreed to take us and fetch us, so we can drink as much as we like as we're not driving."

The thought of drink and me getting drunk again whirled around in my head and I almost felt nauseous just thinking about it, but Morgan seemed excited.

Our evening was quite an event in the sense that I never got drunk, but Morgan certainly got merry, so much so that I had to help him get into and out of Mr Govender's car when we came home and also had to help him undress for bed.

I must admit that the company was pleasant and so was the music. It wasn't excessively loud like the time that I had gone with Alvin and Sarisha, but it was fun to watch Morgan dancing with everyone, myself included.

Back at the house, I tried to get him to quieten down so we wouldn't wake Neelan's mother, but the more we tried to get him to calm down, the more he giggled and sang. Fortunately Mr Govender saw the funny side to Morgan's behaviour and didn't reprimand him. In our bedroom, he fell onto his bed and continued singing while I tried to quieten him down.

"Sh, Morgan. Come, you must get undressed and into bed."

"I can't," he laughed.

"What do you mean you can't?"

"I can't get my clothes off; you'll have to help me."

I slipped off his shoes and socks then unbuttoned his shirt. I tried to lift his shoulders off the bed so that I could slip his shirt off, but found the going tough as he was like a dead weight. Eventually I managed to get his shirt off. Then it was the matter of trying to undo his jeans. I unzipped them and tugged and pulled at them, but they never moved.

"Lift your hips so I can get your jeans off."

Morgan tried to lift his hips from the bed, but it took such an effort that I had to be quick before his body collapsed back on the bed, with him giggling. After much tugging, I managed to get his jeans down to his ankles and then slip them from him. He lay there in his white underpants, giggling. The next step was to try to get him covered but by lying on the blankets, made it difficult for me to cover him.

"Unless you help me, I'm not going to be able to cover you, Morgan," I said, trying to pull the blankets from underneath him.

Eventually I gave up and took one of the blankets on my bed and threw it over his semi-naked body.

"Right, now go to sleep and I'll see you in the morning," I said, as I began to undress.

Once I had undressed, I switched off the bedroom light and peace reigned over us, at least for five minutes and then a voice murmured from the other side of the room.

"I'm cold, Raj."

I heaved a sigh and got out of bed.

"Well if you'd only move I could get you under your blankets, but you're too heavy to move."

"Snuggle in here and that will get me warm," he muttered.

I hesitated and thought of the two of us huddled together in the same bed and wondered whether I should do that. I grabbed another blanket from my bed and moved back to Morgan's bed, climbed in next to him and threw the blanket over us. I could feel his firm body next to mine and I could feel the coldness that he was experiencing. I snuggled as close as I could to him and let some of my warmth spread to him. He turned to face me and I felt an arm wrap around my waist. We were now lying face-to-face and our bodies were pressed tightly together. I could feel myself becoming aroused by his touch and I thought maybe I should climb from his bed and return to my own, but the closeness made me feel secure and safe. It wasn't long before I felt Morgan's own arousal pressing against me as his arm tightened around my waist.

The following morning we awoke in our separate beds, but he never made mention of what took place in his bed during the night. I chose not to raise the topic as it might embarrass him.

"Hi, how are you feeling this morning? Any hangover?"

"Ooh! My head aches a bit, but I think I'll survive," he replied.

"Good. Go and have a cold shower and I'm sure that will wake you up and refresh you," I suggested, getting out of bed and beginning to pack my suitcase.

"What time is your brother coming to fetch us, Morgan?"

"He was coming early because he had an appointment in Durban at about 11:00am."

We showered, dressed, had breakfast and just before 9:00am, Clinton arrived to fetch us. We said our goodbyes and thanked Neelan and his Mum for having us there and soon we were back on the road heading for Durban.

CHAPTER 15

The holidays were over and everyone was back at school, but I hadn't told Sarisha about my week in Pietermaritzburg with Morgan, just in case she became jealous and chose to punish me by not talking to me. However, I had also noticed that on our first day back at school, Morgan hadn't spoken to me, but then I thought perhaps he was busy with his sporting friends.

At first break, I and Sarisha sat in our usual spot chatting about the holidays and life in general, when we saw Morgan. Sarisha waved and called him over saying that she wanted to ask him about his holiday. I hoped, in desperation, that he wouldn't say anything about the two of us being together, because I really didn't want to upset Sarisha.

"Hi there, good-looking. How was your holiday?" she asked as he neared us.

Morgan smiled at her, but seemed to give me a blank stare.

"It was fine thanks, and yours?"

"I just stayed at home and didn't do much. Did you go away at all?"

I looked desperately at Morgan as if to suggest that he lie for me.

"Yes, I went to my cousin's place in Pietermaritzburg."

"That must have been boring; there's nothing to do there."

"Not at all. I had a wonderful time."

Morgan still never smiled at me and I wondered what I had done to deserve this treatment. I wondered whether he was embarrassed by our sleeping together, but he not said anything to me about it.

"Is your cousin older or younger than you?'

"We're pretty much the same age," replied Morgan.

"And did you meet any interesting people while you were there?" continued Sarisha with her interrogation.

"Yep, a few."

Then Sarisha turned to me.

"By the way Raj, your mother said that you had gone away. Where did you go, because you didn't say anything to me before you left?"

I felt trapped. Morgan now looked desperately at me as though it was my turn to lie.

"I just went to a friend's place on the coast," I offered, trying not to make eye-contact with Morgan. "Why, did you miss me?"

"Of course I missed you. In fact I missed both of you," replied Sarisha.

"Listen guys, I must go," said Morgan excusing himself from our company. "I'll probably see you later."

He hurriedly sped off towards some of his friends and I couldn't help thinking that perhaps I had said something or done something to offend him. I felt a little hurt by his approach to me, but I thought I'd get Morgan alone later and find out what the problem was. I also felt terrible that I had lied in front of Morgan.

At lunch break, it was again Sarisha and me together and no Morgan, but I did see one of his friends and asked him if they had any sports practice after school, because I thought I might catch him then. They were apparently having swimming coaching that afternoon, so I figured I'd wait for Morgan after school, but not tell Sarisha I'd be staying late.

The bell for the end of the school day rang and I hurried to the change rooms where I knew the boys would be going to prepare for swimming practice. I didn't frequent these change rooms often as I wasn't as keen on sport as Morgan was, but when I entered the building it had a cold, musty smell to it. In the change room itself there were lockers and rows of benches, some hooks on the walls for people to hang items on and then at one end were toilets and showers. I soon heard voices approaching and wondered whether I should hide or wait outside. I didn't want to embarrass Morgan than I might have already, so I chose to sit in one of the toilet cubicles and when I came out I would say that I needed the toilet urgently, that was why I was in the change room, should anyone question me.

The approaching voices got louder until I could hear everyone chatting quite happily to one another as they got undressed. Amongst these voices, I heard Morgan's and could hear him telling someone about his week's holiday in Pietermaritzburg.

"Did you get any girls while you were there?" I heard someone ask.

"Sure!" came Morgan's reply.

"And did you score?"

"What do you think?"

There was a loud raucous laugh from the group. I sat in the toilet listening to their conversations and wondering when I should make my appearance.

"Was she hot?" asked one of the voices.

"Nothing like we've got here in Durbs," I heard Morgan reply.

"Are you going to see her again?" asked the voice.

"I don't know. You know it was like one of those one-night-stands," answered Morgan.

I sat dejectedly on the toilet seat listening to his fabrication. Obviously he was trying to impress his friends, but then I wondered if he would lie to me like he was doing to his friends, but then I remembered that I had lied to him in front of Sarisha. I decided I had heard enough, so I stood up, flushed the toilet and opened the door. Everyone turned to see who had been in the toilet. My eyes caught Morgan's and he stood staring with a horrified look on his face, obviously knowing that I had heard everything that had been said between him and one of the other boys.

"Hi there. What are you doing here?" asked one of Morgan's friends.

"I had to use the toilet urgently and this was the nearest one," I retorted, walking past the group but keeping a firm eye on Morgan to see his reaction.

As I exited the change room building, I glanced back and saw Morgan still watching me, but I kept walking to the bus stop.

As I sat on the bus heading home, I wanted to cry but something inside of me prevented that from happening. A part of me felt cheated, yet another part of me was glad that I had heard their conversation because it opened my eyes to the lies and deception that some people offer. When I got home I shut myself in my room and lay on my bed thinking about my first day back at school's experience. I knew that I couldn't call on Sarisha for comfort because if I did, she would have to know about Morgan and my week in Pietermaritzburg, and I didn't want that to happen. My mind was in turmoil because I had heard the fabrication that Morgan had made in the change room, but I also was fully aware that I had said I spent my holiday at the coast, when in fact I'd been nowhere there. Was I just as bad as Morgan in telling the truth?

"Raj, are you all right?" asked my mother, knocking on my bedroom door.

"Yes Amah."

"Can I come in?" she asked.

I knew that I couldn't say 'no' because then she would suspect something.

"Come in," I shouted through the door to her.

My mother came in and sat on the edge of my bed and took hold of my hand.

"What is the matter my child?"

The tone of her voice was so soothing that I felt I wanted to cry instantly.

"Oh, it's nothing much Amah."

"Has something happened to you or has someone hurt you in any way?"

"Amah, it's nothing that you should worry about. I'm fine. Really I am."

"My child, if you want to talk about it, you must tell me."

"Yes Amah. Thank you Amah."

My mother got up from the bed and made her way to the bedroom door, but before she left, she turned to me once more and said, "If it's love, these things will happen often in your life, but don't let it get you down."

With that, my mother left my room closing the door behind her. How did she know about love? Had someone said something to her about my feelings for Morgan or Peter? Maybe she hadn't thought about Morgan or Peter, but thought I might have found a girlfriend or something. I lay on my bed for some time, pondering on both her behaviour and that of Morgan.

That evening, after I and my brothers had eaten our dinner, the phone rang and my mother called me to the phone.

"There's a young man on the line, my child."

I wondered whether it was Morgan and if so, should I answer or not. I stood holding the receiver in my hand not knowing what to do while my mother watched me.

"Hello," I said, my voice soft and quivering.

"Hi Raj, it's Morgan here."

"Oh, hi!" was all I could muster up to say, and then without enthusiasm.

"Listen, I'm sorry about what happened in the change room today, but I didn't know you were there."

I thought this was a lame excuse. He would no doubt have said the same things had I been there or not.

"Look, I can't talk now," I said, seeing my mother still watching me and obviously listening.

"Can I meet you after school tomorrow to explain?"

"If you want to, but I don't think you have to offer me an explanation; you need to look to yourself instead."

There was a stunned silence at the other end of the line and I wondered if I'd been too harsh on Morgan.

"Listen, I really am sorry. I'll speak to you tomorrow?"

"Sure," I replied and put down the phone.

"Everything all right?" asked my mother as she stood watching my reactions.

"Yes, thank you, Amah."

After my phone call, I made my way back to my room, only to be disturbed about two hours later by my father who burst into my room. I knew that he'd been drinking again and I would probably be his punching bag for some reason totally unconnected to me or my brothers, but because of something that probably happened at work. This was often his course of action. He came in swearing, followed closely by my mother who was there to defend me, no doubt.

"People are talking about you," he screamed, shaking his fist at me.

"I don't know what you're talking about Apah. What people?"

"People are saying you're not normal."

"What!" exclaimed my mother. "There is nothing wrong with our child. He's as normal as the next one. What rubbish is this that you are sprouting?"

"I heard you like boys," shouted my father, striking me across the face and sending me flying onto the bedroom floor.

"Stop this," screamed my mother, coming to my assistance.

"Leave him," shouted my father. "He's a disgrace to our family name."

I lay cowering on the bedroom floor as my father ranted and raved like a lunatic above me. I felt the hefty foot of my father as he kicked at my stomach and my ribs. My mother started trying to drag him away from me, shouting at him at the same time, but he pushed her aside and continued to kick at my prone body, landing blows on my legs, face and stomach. I crumpled up into a foetus position and I could feel the pain race through my body with each blow and the warm trickle of blood as it oozed from my nose and mouth. Soon my brothers, who had come into my room to see what the commotion was, began to cry when they saw my father attacking me, but my mother continued to try to pull my father away from me by hitting him, only to receive his retaliatory blows.

"Get out! Get out of my fucking house! You are nothing but shit! I don't want filth in my house! Get out you bastard!" screamed my father, giving me another almighty kick in the chest and then storming from the bedroom and leaving my mother, brothers and me all in tears.

First I had been disappointed by Morgan's comments and the way he ostracised me at school and now I was being abused by my father who was accusing me of something I knew to be true, but which still upset me. Why couldn't he accept me for who I was? Just because I liked boys didn't make me a murderer or something equally bad. My mind was in turmoil. I loved my parents but I liked boys as well and was now being made to feel inferior by my father.

I lay on the floor quivering and crying, the tears mingling with the blood already covering my face. I was crying from both the pain and the humiliation. I was also shocked to think that my father could treat his child in this manner. My mother came and knelt next to me on the floor, cradling my head. My body ached and my lips felt as though they were growing in size from where he had punched and hit me.

"I will go away," I sobbed as I lay on the floor, blood running from a cut above my eye, my split lip and from my nose.

"Hush my child," said my mother in between sobs as she tried to comfort me and wipe away the blood. "Do not be silly. Where will you go?"

"I'll go. I'll go now," I sobbed, trying to get up slowly from the floor.

I raised myself with the help of my mother, hobbled as I stood and found my balance, then I walked slowly from my room, bent over from the pain in my stomach and ribs, towards the front door, with my mother sobbing behind me, and watching anxiously as I approached the front door. My father sat fuming and cursing in the lounge, calling me all the uncouth names he could think of, and with a large glass of Whiskey in his hand. I opened the front door and wandered aimlessly out into the darkness and hobbled slowly down the street towards Sarisha's house. My mother never ventured out of the house, but I know she stood in the doorway and watched. I don't know if it was instinct that led me to Sarisha's house, but when I reached her house, I knocked gently on their front door. After a while, Sarisha's mother opened it and gasped as she saw the blood streaked face looking at her.

"Raj, is that you? Oh my God, what happened? Come in. Sarisha, bring me water quickly," she called out.

Sarisha came to the door when she heard her mother's call. Both women were shocked by what they saw; blood oozing from my face. I was helped into their kitchen where mother and daughter sponged my face to clean it of the blood. I could feel my eye beginning to puff up and I knew that I'd have a black eye when the swelling went down, and I knew that my lips were already swollen.

"Was this that father of yours again?" asked Sarisha, angrily.

"Don't worry, child, you're safe here and at least your mother knows that you'll be safe here. Tomorrow you stay here and you're not going to school."

"I have to," I sobbed. I knew that I had to speak to Morgan and I must go to school.

"You're going to look a sad sight tomorrow, Raj. My mother's right, you should stay here tomorrow to allow the swelling to subside a little, and to rest," said Sarisha.

I knew that it was pointless arguing with these two women, and letting Morgan wait for a day or two before speaking to him might be a good thing for both of us. It may make him think a little.

A bed was prepared for me and after having been cleaned up, I was put to bed where I slept peacefully throughout the night until the early morning when Sarisha brought in a hot cup of tea for me before she left for school.

"Ooh!" said Sarisha when she saw my face. "I'm sorry to say this, but I wouldn't go out with you looking like that." Then she burst out laughing.

I felt hurt by her laughter, but I was sure it was meant more to humour me than to hurt me.

My whole body ached when I moved and I was glad that they had decided for me that I shouldn't go to school – I doubt I would have been able to do anything because I was so stiff and sore.

Most of the day I slept but about lunchtime my mother came to see that I was in good hands. She kept apologising for my father's behaviour, but I knew it was because of the drink and that it wasn't her fault. She sat on the edge of my bed, but at no time did she mention the words that my father had uttered. At no time did she say I was a disgrace to her and at no time did she mention the word 'boys'. After spending half an hour with me, she went back home and I remained in bed.

When Sarisha returned from school she brought Morgan with her.

"I'm so sorry to hear what happened to you, Raj. Sarisha told me at school and I asked if it would be OK for me to come home with her to see you."

Now I had mixed feelings. Was he genuinely concerned about my well-being, or was he only seeking sympathy from me for the lies he'd been saying to his friends?

Deep down I was pleased to see him, but I also felt hurt. I could feel tears beginning to well-up in my eyes, but I didn't want Sarisha to see them, so I asked her if she could leave Morgan and me alone so that we could talk. She seemed a little suspicious, but agreed to do as I asked. She left the room and closed the bedroom door behind her. In case she was standing outside of the door, listening, I chose to speak softly to Morgan.

"Morgan, why did you ignore me at school when we got back?"

He seemed unsure of himself and somewhat embarrassed.

"Was it something I said or did to you to upset you in that way?"

"No, nothing."

"Then what was it?"

"Raj, it's my fault."

"What's your fault?"

"You know the last night at Neelan's, when I got drunk…?"

"Yes? What about it?"

"We slept together…"

"So?'

"I've never slept with another boy before and I'm embarrassed that I might have done something that I shouldn't have."

I hesitated for a moment before resuming our discussion.

"You mean have sex with a boy?"

Morgan seemed struck by the word 'sex' when I mentioned it.

"Um, yes… if you put it like that," he cautiously replied.

"Morgan, if something happened, then perhaps it was meant to happen. I like you and you said that you liked me, so what's so wrong with us showing our feelings to each other?"

"But my parents have said that it's bad for boys to make it with each other."

"That's what your parents say, but what do you say? Is it something you liked or disliked? So often we do exactly what our parents say, and not what we really want, so what do you want?"

"I don't know."

"What I remember of that night, I enjoyed, and as I've said before, I like you very much," I continued.

"But?"

"There has to be a 'But!' somewhere there?"

"But… my parents say it's wrong. I've heard them say that," said Morgan.

"So I take it that you're going to marry some poor girl one day just so that your parents can proudly say they are grandparents, but behind your girlfriend's back, you'll probably be sneaking off with the odd boy to enjoy your pleasures. Is that what you see for yourself in the future?"

Morgan remained quiet as he took in what I had said.

"I'm sorry it sounds so harsh, but I think that is what your reality is going to be like when you marry. You are gay like me, but the sad thing is that you are going to ruin some girl's life just to please your family and its name, instead of doing things to bring happiness to you. Is that what you really want?"

Morgan was dumbstruck by my words. I could see that he too had tears welling up in his eyes as the words stung like driving rain. It was not my intention to hurt him, but I wanted him to be happy and to be himself, but I could see that he was torn between himself and his family name. He took hold of my hand and gently gave it a squeeze.

"I'm sorry," he said, choking back the tears.

I wasn't sure whether this was meant to be an apology or he was sorry because he was going to follow the family name route, but either way, my feelings for Morgan wouldn't change; I liked him.

He took control of his emotions and wiped away the tears, then stood up, smiled at me and said he should go and catch the bus home.

"Maybe I'll see you at school tomorrow," I said as he left and Sarisha returned.

"Are things OK?" enquired Sarisha.

"Fine thanks," I replied, feeling that my heart was lighter for having spoken to Morgan.

CHAPTER 16

While I was at Sarisha's house, my mother had apparently tried to talk some sense into my father's drunken head. She had taken the opportunity to say something to him whilst I was away, hoping that the tension between father and son might dissipate. She sat him down in our lounge and tried to understand her husband of years.

When I returned home after leaving Sarisha's house, I could see that my mother was upset and I sat down with her and asked what the problem was. She told me she had spoken to my father in an effort to get him to accept me as I was.

"What did you say?" I asked.

"I asked him why he had to speak to you like that," my mother replied.

"And what did he say?"

She hung her head and remained silent for a while, and then she looked at me with sadness in her eyes.

"He told me to shut up," was her answer.

I looked shocked by this revelation, but my mother continued. "He said he was sick and tired of the way that I protected you and that you were…" she broke off as if unable to repeat the words.

"I was a what?" I asked, determined to hear what my father thought of me.

"My child, it hurts me to say these things."

I could see her embarrassment and that she probably regretted having started this conversation, but I persisted in finding out…

"He said you were … were an embarrassment to our family. I am so sorry, my child," said my mother, hugging me to her bosom.

I could see that my mother had been shocked at being told to 'shut up' as my father had never said that to her before, either when he was drunk or sober. Added to that, my mother seemed shocked by the attitude my father had towards me.

"I tried to get him to understand how cruel he'd been to you by calling you all those names; names I have never heard him use before. It hurt me, my child and I asked if he had forgotten that you are his son."

"What did he say?" I asked.

"He said he hadn't forgotten but he felt that the son he had was no longer the son he had now. He said you were different."

"I asked him what he meant by 'different' but he only grunted. You know what he's like sometimes."

I nodded knowingly. I had found that whenever my father became drunk, he became ruder, however, my mother continued to tell me what had happened.

"I asked him about those names and where he had got them from, and he merely said that people were talking."

"What people?" I implored.

There was a moment of silence as my mother looked at me in her arms

"He couldn't answer me," continued my mother, "because he knew they were lies and that it was the drink speaking and not him and then he swore at me."

"He swore at you!" I exclaimed in horror. I had never heard my father swear.

"They were horrible words," said my mother, not mentioning them to me.

"I told him that you were his blood and flesh, no matter what he might think. I was so angry that I even told him that I was sick of his drinking and the embarrassment that he brought to this family. He always thinks that he is big in front of his friends, but in fact he was nothing when he was drunk."

"He embarrasses me when he is drunk," I replied.

We clung to each other and I could feel my mother's breathing, heaving as she spoke. I could sense her anger and frustration at my father.

"What did he do then, Amah?"

She told me that they had shouted at each, the sound reverberating around the lounge, then they fell silent and they stared coldly at each other, neither saying anything more.

"Did you not do anything?" I enquired.

"No. Suddenly he rose from where he had been sitting and made his way into the kitchen and poured himself another drink. He flung himself back into his chair, spilling some of his drink in the process, and resumed his glaring at me," said my mother.

"Did he say anything to you?"

"He simply said that he would drink as much as he wanted and that I could do nothing about it. He said he was the man of the house so he would do as he pleased."

My mother was beginning to have tears in her eyes as she told me of my father's attitude.

"I try to be a good wife and mother to you children," said my mother weeping gently, "but he seems to ignore all the things I do for him and children."

"Did you tell him that?" I asked, trying to wipe her tears away with my hand.

She nodded.

"And what did he say?"

"He asked me what my problem was, as he had married me for precisely that reason, to look after him and the children I had."

Her weeping became more intense, tears streaming down her cheeks. "After all that I have done for him and the family, he speaks to me as if I am one from a lower caste. Maybe I too would be better off leaving this house."

"No! No, Amah," I pleaded.

"Well that's what he suggested."

"That you leave?" I asked with shock.

"And take you and the small ones with me as well, but if I went, he'd see to it that I never returned to this house again."

The threat of exclusion hung heavily over my mother and the shock at being told she was welcome to leave affected my mother. Neither she nor I had ever heard my father speak in this manner before, nor had he ever threatened to banish her from the home.

"But Amah, you can't do that." The thought of us out on the street was a frightening idea.

My mother told me that she wasn't sure whether my father would rescind his threats or whether she would find herself out on the streets along with four young children. Her obvious thought was not to be on the streets, but then she tried to rationalise her situation and thought that if my father passed out from the alcohol, he might forget what had happened and apologise to her for speaking in such a harmful way, when he had sobered up the next day. On the other hand, he might very well remember everything that had gone between them and remind her that his threat was not in jest or in a moment of madness, but that he had meant every word.

"Amah, why does he drink so much?"

My mother hesitated on being asked this question. Prior to this event I had never thought as to why my father drank so much. I was aware that drinking for social reasons was common, but it seemed that my father drank to excess.

My mother thought for a while as if to find the answer or the right words to explain.

"Maybe it's my fault," she replied, quietly.

"Why is it your fault?"

"My child, I have four beautiful children and I'm so grateful for having all of you, but you see now I am unable to have any more children."

"Why?"

"Shall we say that I'm too old to have children now?"

"But you're not old, Amah."

"Thank you my child," and for the first time I saw a slight smile on my mother's face.

"But what has that to do with Apah?"

"He would like more children and I cannot have them so he gets angry sometimes and I think that is why he turns to drink."

By this time, my young brothers, Niven and Krishna, had entered the lounge where my mother and I were and stood staring at the tears running down my mother's cheeks. Not fully understanding, they both began to cry, causing my mother to pick them both up in her arms and hurry them off to my bedroom.

I remained in the lounge, thinking about the whole event that had taken place and how this might affect both my mother and me. One thing I knew about my father and his drinking was that once he had succumbed to the effects of Bacchus, he would quietly fall asleep and we would leave him where he was until he awoke in his own time.

CHAPTER 17

My days at school after having left Sarisha's house were spent trying to avoid too much eye contact with people as my eyes were a glorious dark purple from the kicks I had received from my father. I had returned to my own home, but my father avoided me like some contaminating plague. My mother had become surprisingly subdued and very little conversation took place between any of us. Even my baby brothers said nothing about my appearance, which surprised me as they spent most of their life firing questions at people.

At school, Morgan had taken the trouble to approach me and enquire as to my well being. He even plucked up the courage to ask what had caused the ruckus between me and my father. I decided that I should tell him the truth, even if it was possibly to my own detriment.

"My father accused me of liking boys and bringing disrespect to the family name," I said, waiting to see Morgan's reaction.

He looked a little shocked that someone would go to the extremes that my father went to, to admonish his child for the sake of the family name.

"You mean he beat you up because you liked boys?"

I nodded my head.

"That's shocking," replied Morgan, not knowing what else to say.

"I suppose when you look at me like this, it's enough to put you off liking boys, hey? Maybe marrying might be the best thing for you to do."

I know there was probably a tone of sarcasm in my voice when I said it, but I was angry. I'm not sure who the actual cause of my anger was, whether it was my father, Morgan or the system, but for reasons unbeknown to me, I was venting my anger on Morgan.

"Raj, don't be so hard on me. I said I was sorry, but I have to come to terms with myself before I can either judge or criticise others. I'm going through that mixed-up stage where I don't know what I want. I'm sure that you've been through that stage, but between you and me, I know that deep down I like boys, but I keep thinking it's going to be a stage that I'll grow out of."

"In other words you think it will go away like a cold might, and then all will be well? I don't think so. Morgan, I can't offer you any more advice. I've tried to explain my situation and you can either accept me or reject me as I am, but I can't change who I am for others, just as I don't expect you to change yourself for others. If you must change in any way, then it must be for you alone, and not for any other reason. Pleasing people for the sake of gaining their gratitude or admiration is a waste of time, but pleasing for yourself is worth it. No matter what your choice in life, I want you to know that I'll always be a friend to you, whether you have any relationship with me or not."

"That means a great deal to me, Raj and I appreciate your candidness and honesty with me."

We shook hands, remaining hold on to each other a little longer than most people might shake hands, but there was a bond running through us as we did so, and then Morgan went his way, probably to his friends.

Although I had been angry, there was just something about Morgan that made everything seem OK. I couldn't remain angry for long with him.

At the end of the week, I decided that I should phone Peter and find out how his tour to the Cape had been.

After school on the Friday, I made my way to the telephone booth and put my money in the tickey box. Peter answered and when I heard his friendly voice, I felt a surge of happiness in me.

"Hi Peter, it's Raj. I just phoned to find out how your tour was and how you are."

"Hi, Raj. I'm fine thanks and the tour was brilliant. We had good weather in Cape Town and we were lucky to win all our matches, but how are you?"

"I'm fine, thanks, but that's fantastic that you guys won your matches," I said excitedly. "But more importantly, when am I going to see you again?"

Silence fell along the telephone line.

"Peter, did you hear me?"

"Yes, I heard you."

"So when am I going to see you?"

"Raj, I think it's going to be a bit awkward at the moment. I'm very busy at school and I have to focus on my studies."

"Sure, I know what you mean. I should be doing the same. You know, Indian parents always put a lot of pressure on us kids to do well in school and I suppose I should be spending more time in my books, but I would like to see you soon."

"Let me give you a call when I'm free," suggested Peter.

I never thought anything of Peter's remark other than we both should be studying, so I was quite happy to accept his idea. We spoke a little more on his tour and what he thought of Cape Town and its people and then we hung up.

When I reached home after my call to Peter, Aunty Selvie was waiting to see me. She had heard from my mother about my father's attack on me and had hurried over to see if her favourite nephew was okay. When she saw me she hugged me tightly and asked if I was in pain.

"I'm fine thanks Aunty, just a little stiff and achy."

She smiled at me and said, "You look like a little squirrel with acorns stuffed in its cheeks, they're so puffy, and those eyes, you must tell me where you got that eye shadow from so that I can get some."

I knew that she was trying to humour me by saying these things and I appreciated her fun approach. She always tried to make awkward situations, light. At no stage did she admonish my father's behaviour, but one thing that really concerned me, required me having to ask her who had said something to my father about me liking boys.

"My darling, I can promise you it wasn't me; however, you must understand that parents often go on intuition. Perhaps no-one said anything to him, but he felt that because you don't have a girlfriend, then you must be gay. Personally that type of thinking shows a very limited mind, but I don't think anyone has told him anything."

"You mean he was just taking a chance?"

"Yes, possibly. You must also understand that when someone has been drinking excessively like him, they often don't know what they say, but that doesn't mean that we can condone his behaviour towards you. Has he spoken to you since the event?"

"No," I replied, hanging my head, not in shame, but in disappointment.

"Don't worry about it. You have a strong mother who'll protect you, and you know that you can call on Uncle Harry and me anytime."

"Thank you Aunty."

"Now, let you and me go and have a quiet chat alone in your room, away from prying ears," said Aunty Selvie, noticing my inquisitive brothers were hovering near to us.

We made our way to my room and closed the door then settled down on my bed.

"I believe you went away for a week. Did you enjoy yourself?"

"Very much, thanks. We went to Pietermaritzburg, Morgan and me. We stayed with his cousin, Neelan."

"And how are things between you and Morgan?"

Again I hung my head, and Aunty Selvie noticed.

"Is there a problem there?"

"He's very mixed up aunty. He said that he also likes boys but his parents seem to be putting pressure on him to conform and find a girlfriend, but I said he was not being true to himself."

"Maybe he's not, Raj, but he must find that out for himself. Sometimes people don't like to be told things, even if it is the truth. And how does he feel about you, did he say?"

"He said that he liked me."

"That's wonderful, my darling."

I hesitated as I wondered whether I should tell Aunty Selvie what happened in Pietermaritzburg.

"One night we slept together, aunty."

Only after I'd said it did I realise how bluntly I had said it.

"Oh!" replied Aunty Selvie somewhat taken aback.

I could see that she didn't know what to say, but just as I was about to say something, she interrupted.

"Darling, you don't have to fill me in with all the details. But how did he react the next day?"

"He was embarrassed, but then we had a talk and I think we sorted out that problem. His main problem is coming to terms with what society expects of him and what he wants in society."

"And your other friend, Peter; have you heard from him?"

"I spoke to him after school today on the phone. He's fine and he had a nice tour to the Cape and said that they won all their matches, but he said we shouldn't see each other because we must prepare for exams at the end of the year."

"Quite right," answered Aunty Selvie. "However, Raj, don't be too disappointed if you don't see Peter as much as you would like. You must understand that he has to face his problems too."

I wasn't quite sure what problems Aunty Selvie was referring to, but I accepted her advice as I knew that she was wise and I trusted her.

"You haven't heard any more about the tickets to see the show at the university have you?" I asked

"Oh yes. Michael has given me tickets so who would you like to go with you?"

I gave it some thought, and then I answered, "May Sarisha come with me, aunty?"

"Of course. You can take whomever you like and if it's Sarisha, so be it."

I had decided that Sarisha had been faithful to me, especially when my father had attacked me, and with Peter and Morgan so undecided about themselves, I decided to take the one person who knew exactly who she was.

After we had completed our little chat together, Aunty Selvie and I emerged from my room and went into the lounge where my mother was busy playing with my brothers. I was always pleased to have Aunty Selvie around and she made me feel happy and content. The fact that I had chosen to take Sarisha to the play also made me feel good inside.

"Amah, can I run down to Sarisha's to tell her that she can come with us to the play?"

"Of course, my child. I'm sure she'll be very pleased to attend the show."

I hurried down the street and soon reached Sarisha's house where I told her of our planned evening.

"But didn't you want to take Peter with you?" she asked.

"That doesn't matter. I asked Aunty Selvie if you could come and she agreed, so it's going to be you and me. I hope you're going to like the show," I coyly added.

When the night of the show dawned, both Sarisha and I were smartly dressed and waited at our house for Uncle Harry and Aunty Selvie to fetch us. There was an air of excitement between the two of us and we had heated discussions about the play and what we expected from it.

"How well do you know the play?" asked Sarisha.

"Hm, not too well, but I know that it's very funny."

"I think it would be even funnier if a man played the part of Lady Bracknell," suggested Sarisha.

"Why is that?" I queried.

"She's such a character and her lines are so funny, that I think it would be even funnier if a man did it."

Having very little knowledge of the play, it still puzzled me why a man should play a female part.

Our discussion was cut short by the arrival of Uncle Harry and Aunty Selvie, both looking very smart and beautiful, respectively.

"Shoo, but your aunty looks beautiful," whispered Sarisha to me when they entered the lounge.

I agreed whole heartedly, but then I knew that Aunty Selvie always looked classy and I always felt proud to be in her company, probably just as proud as Uncle Harry must have felt about her. We climbed into their car, waved goodbye to my mother and headed off to the University of Natal.

When we arrived at the theatre on the campus, Michael was there with Vanesh to meet us. I introduced them to Sarisha and both men hugged me when they saw me.

"It's so good to see you again, Raj," said Michael. "How have you been?"

"Very well thanks, Michael."

"How's the love-life?" he whispered to me.

I giggled and probably blushed in the dark.

"Not too hot, I'm afraid, but I'm sure that one day I'll find someone like you found Vanesh."

"You're right there, but don't just take anyone, search for the best."

I was glad that they were Aunty Selvie's friends because I found them both so interesting, and I respected their openness. We made our way into the theatre and found our seats. I looked around to survey the scene and noticed only a few Whites in the audience. It was clear that the majority of the audience were Indians.

As I was seated between Michael and Aunty Selvie, I leaned towards her and whispered, "How come there are Whites and Indians here together? I thought it was against the law?"

She smiled and winked at Michael who had overheard me.

"It's one of those crazy features of our land," she replied. "You see the University is considered private property and therefore they can have performances for Indians or Whites and really the police can't raid here."

"So it's OK for us and Michael to be seated together?"

"Very much so," said Michael, nudging me.

It felt so good to be able to sit together as an integrated group without the feeling of intimidation or threat hanging over one's head all the time. The lights dimmed and some background music started. Once the theatre lights were out, the curtains on the stage opened and there was Michael's beautifully designed set depicting a grand lounge. The audience burst into spontaneous applause on seeing the set and its décor. I think Michael felt proud of his work.

"It's beautiful," I whispered to Michael, and I felt him squeeze my arm.

The show started and soon everyone was laughing heartily at the clever dialogue and the comic situations that arose. Lady Bracknell, whom I had waited for all night, after Sarisha and my discussions, proved to be a towering woman whom Aunty Selvie likened to a Wagnerian opera singer.

"What do you mean by that aunty?" I enquired.

"Large breasted and domineering," she whispered back, causing Michael to smile at her comment.

Out of the corner of my eye I could see how Sarisha was enjoying herself. She was seated between Michael and Vanesh and I could see that she was often in discussion with Vanesh.

When interval arrived, we all went outside to get a little fresh air, as the theatre never had air-conditioning and it was becoming stuffy inside.

"How are you enjoying the show, Sarisha?" asked Michael.

"I love it," she squealed with delight. "It's so well acted and your sets are magnificent."

"Well, they're not just mine; Vanesh and I worked on them together. I couldn't have done them alone. I'm the designer and he's the artist."

"What he means is he does the drawings and I do the work," quipped Vanesh.

Poor Sarisha was enjoying the show so much, she actually felt offended at having to have an interval.

"I wished they just carried on without a break," she said sadly. "I think the interval breaks the illusion and when we go back inside, we're going to have to start all over again to get back into the feeling of the play."

I thought she had a valid point, but as Michael pointed out, the actors needed a rest. While we were enjoying the fresh air, a bell suddenly sounded, alerting us and warning us that we should return to the theatre in order to see the second half of the show.

The second half of the show was equally funny and good, and both Sarisha and I were often on the edges of our seats, totally immersed in the action taking place on stage.

At the end of the show, the cast received a resounding applause from the audience and as we made our way out of the theatre, we thanked Michael for the tickets. I had thoroughly enjoyed my evening and I knew from the laughter coming from Sarisha, that she had too.

We said our goodnights to Michael and Vanesh and this time both Sarisha and I got hugs from the two men.

"I like them," whispered Sarisha to me as we made our way to Uncle Harry's car.

"So do I," I answered.

As we drove home, Aunty Selvie was discussing the play with us and explained something that I had not thought of as I watched the play.

"You know how I explained to you, Raj, the way people are prejudiced and how they often pre-judge others before getting to know them, well there was an element of that in the play tonight."

"Where aunty?"

"If you think back to the scene with Lady Bracknell and Mr Worthing when she is interrogating him regarding the potential marriage, if you listen to the questions that she asks, there's an element of prejudice in them although it's very funny. She asks him who his parents are, obviously to decide if he is worthy of her ward's hand, and then asks him where he was born…"

"Oh, I liked the way he said he was born in a handbag," I laughed.

"Yes, but did you notice how he tried to explain the type of handbag? In other words he was saying it was made of leather, suggesting that it wasn't an ordinary handbag but something special, like him."

"I see," I replied, "But what is your point?"

"Just as we have preconceived ideas in our culture, so it is found in others as well. Just as Indian parents want their children to marry good partners, they also want something special for themselves. They don't want an in-law who might not come up to their standards and therefore they develop judgemental attitudes. The same applies to the Apartheid regime. They are prejudiced in the sense that they don't want their race or culture relating to or interacting with the other races because they have pre-judged them and feel that they are inferior. Raj, as a young boy, you must understand a very important point, and that is that children are nor born with prejudice; they get it from adults."

"So are you saying that Lady Bracknell was prejudiced?"

"In the sense that she wanted only the best for her ward, no matter what the person's feelings were. Put your father into the position of Lady Bracknell and you'll see that perhaps the reason why he abuses you is that what he wants is the best for him, without considering your feelings."

"Do you really think he does it because he wants the best for me? I think it's just because he's drunk and he daren't hit Amah or the little ones."

I knew that Aunty Selvie understood exactly what I meant and knew that I was probably right, but she added, "I know that it might sound harsh, but you have to face reality, and for that matter, so must he. I say that if you love someone deeply enough, go and get that person, no matter what others might think or say."

I sat quietly in the car as we drove back pondering on what Aunty Selvie had said both now and previously and things were beginning to make sense to me. I had to be myself and not something someone else wanted and that meant I must get on with my life and let things happen on their own without forcing issues, but I would have to be strong, both in my determination and in maintaining my self-image for the better.

We arrived at Sarisha's house and her mother was waiting up for her. Both she and her mother thanked Uncle Harry and Aunty Selvie profusely for taking her to the theatre and then she gave me a little kiss on the cheek to say thank you for asking her to go along.

We soon arrived back home having dropped off Sarisha. It was late so neither Aunty Selvie nor Uncle Harry wanted to come in for some tea, which I had offered to make, but they waited until I was safely indoors and then they drove off to their home.

I went to bed that night happy in the thought that all of us had enjoyed a most entertaining evening and that it was also nice to have seen and spoken to Michael and Vanesh again, as well as having Aunty Selvie to explain the play and its underlying message to me.

CHAPTER 18

For two weeks after having been to the theatre, both Sarisha and I still continued to talk about the show and how much we had enjoyed it, and during those two weeks, I had not received any phone calls from Peter. I was beginning to wonder whether he was so busy studying that he had forgotten me, and I also wondered whether I should call him and remind him he had promised to phone me, when he was free. One half of me was saying 'phone' while the other half said 'don't force the issue and wait for his call'. If I was meant to get a telephone call from Peter, it would happen, but in the meantime I had ample opportunities to see Morgan at school; however, I also noticed how his lunchtime visits to Sarisha and me seemed to be dwindling.

I wondered whether I had offended Morgan in some way and that was why he was avoiding me, but I wasn't about to ask. I thought if he wanted to inform me on anything, he would make the first move.

One day Morgan did approach me and asked if I was doing anything over the weekend, to which I replied that I wasn't.

"How would you like to go to the beach?"

I had flashes of Peter and me at the beach and what had happened there, and the thought of Morgan and I being at the beach together excited me. Would it be like the time Peter and I were there or would nothing exciting happen? Perhaps I was letting my imaginative mind run away with me, as usual.

"That sounds wonderful," I answered gleefully. "This Saturday?"

"Yes. We can meet there if you like and then perhaps have some lunch together when we're tired of swimming and tanning."

Things seemed to be looking up for me with regard to Morgan's attitude. The fact that he had approached me meant that I couldn't have said nor done anything to upset him in any way.

"What time shall I meet you there and where?" I asked.

"Shall we go to what they call the Coloureds' beach? At least we won't be hassled there."

I knew what Morgan meant by us not being hassled there. We wouldn't have prying eyes from defiant White men who only wanted to humiliate and antagonise non-white people. At least I knew about that, but I wasn't sure whether Morgan had ever experienced that humiliation.

"Sounds great to me," I replied, because I knew we could go to the sand dunes if the wind came up or if we wanted privacy. "What time shall I meet you there?"

"Say 10:00. Will that give you enough time to get from your house to the beach?"

"Ample time. Then is that a date?"

Morgan smiled at my use of the word 'date'.

"Yes, it's a date."

I smiled back happily, but inside, I was a bundle of excitement and didn't want to expose that to Morgan in case he misconstrued my intentions.

"Then I'll see you on Saturday," confirmed Morgan as he left to go back to his friends.

Again this was something that was going to remain private and I wasn't going to tell Sarisha of our plans, in case she decided to come to the beach as well. It wasn't that I had anything against Sarisha and me being with Morgan, but I wanted our time together to be private.

Hoorah! Saturday! My long-awaited visit to the beach!

I was up bright and early putting on my clothes and packing my towel and swimming shorts in my backpack. Although the rest of the family weren't up and about, it didn't stop me from merrily humming to myself as I packed my bag. A sense of excitement filled me and I felt as though I was floating on some puffy white cloud, high in the sky without a care in the world.

I caught the usual Saturday morning bus into the city, with its cargo of gaudily dressed aunties and grannies all going to do their weekly shopping. I sat deep in thought as we travelled, oblivious of the merry chatter emanating from the women. My thoughts focussed only on Morgan and going to the beach with him. Once we arrived in the city, I made the necessary change to another bus and headed towards the beach front. On arrival at the Snake Park area, I alighted, avoided the illustrious toilets where I had encountered that horrific man who called me names, and headed towards the so-called Coloureds' beach and the sand dunes to await Morgan.

I knew that I was a little early, so I strolled casually along the water's edge, letting the broken waves splash my feet and legs. The sea tended to be a tranquil blue and there were very gentle swells, making the sea almost mirror-like as the sun was reflected off it, and its coolness on my feet helped to keep my body temperature at a constant level. When I neared the area that Peter and I usually went to, I headed inland towards the sand dunes where we would lie to avoid any winds blowing and to have privacy. Why I was attracted to that area, I do not know, but I made my way slowly up the sand. The sun was blazing down but that didn't deter me from hurrying over the stinging sand.

I climbed to the top of the sand dunes and stood admiring the view of the sea, stretching before me, just as Peter and I had done before. There were a number of ships anchored off shore, no doubt waiting to be allowed entry into the harbour, and in the tranquillity of the water, they looked like they were paper cut-outs glued to the surface.

As I surveyed the beach front, I noticed that Morgan wasn't in sight yet, so I just stood taking in a gentle breeze that seemed to tickle my face, arms and legs, and the beautiful view. I then turned to look down the dunes where the mangrove bush was and there among the leaves and branches my eye caught sight of something pale blue in colour. I could make out it was a swimming costume, because I soon saw a pair of tanned legs, and then I saw a canary yellow costume and realised that two people were lying among the bushes.

My mind immediately flashed back to the time Peter and I spent time together in the bushes. It excited me and I realised that I missed Peter. I stood watching the blue and yellow swimming costumes for a while and then I decided to venture closer.

I moved slightly to see if I could see who it might be and in doing so, noticed that they were both White men, lying side by side on their towels. Although I couldn't see their faces, I could make out that their bodies were touching and as I watched, so I saw them kissing. I felt a pleasant feeling in my groin as I watched the two people; my voyeuristic behaviour was exciting me. Not satisfied with my slightly obscured view, quietly I edged a little closer in a predatory manner until I was close enough to make out their features. One was blonde while the other had dark hair and the one seemed to be a more mature-looking person of about twenty-five or thereabouts. Their arms were encircling each other's waist and they seemed to be clutching to each other. As I stood watching them, my groin now tingling with excitement at the sight, they moved, and I was able to see their features more clearly. I froze in case they saw me and as I did so, I saw the attractive features of the young man in the pale blue Speedo costume – Peter. He was lying in the arms of the slightly older man.

Although the feeling of excitement was still in my groin, it suddenly began to diminish. A feeling of betrayal, of horror, of anxiety rushed through me like an electric shock. I couldn't believe that I was watching Peter lying with someone else. My mind spun in turmoil, my heart seemed to speed up and I didn't know whether to gasp or cry. I obviously had feelings for Peter but to see him in the arms of another was disturbing for me. I had not experienced this feeling before and wasn't sure how to deal with it. I tried hastily to remind myself that as neither Peter nor I were in any sort of relationship, I couldn't stop him from doing whatever he wanted, but it still upset me to see these two men together. Perhaps now I was beginning to understand how Sarisha might have felt about my friendship with Morgan.

I stood staring at the two men for some time, transfixed in a moment of anxiety. As I stood there mesmerized, I heard a gentle sound behind me and came face-to-face with Morgan standing there.

"What are you watching?" he whispered into my ear.

I couldn't tell him who it was, but he could clearly see the pained look on my face and the two men entwined in each other's arms.

"Check them," he whispered again, with a hint of surprised excitement in his voice. "Do they know you're watching them?"

I didn't answer, but shook my head. Somehow I wanted to flee the scene, but something kept me drawn to their action. I don't know if it was wilful thinking on my part or just plain curiosity, but I couldn't move. I noticed that Morgan seemed to have become quite intrigued by the men's activities and knelt down on the sand to watch. A strange sensation overcame me as I watched the first boy in my life making out with someone else, while the second boy in my life watched them at it.

A feeling of desperation overcame me at that moment as I watched Morgan watching Peter.

"Come!" I said, tugging at Morgan's arm and trying to pull him away.

With our sudden movement and my voice, Peter and his friend stopped and looked up. For a fraction of a second Peter's and my eyes met and I could see the look on his face as he recognised me. He looked surprised and shocked all at once, but I don't think he saw Morgan. However, Peter's friend who was with him shouted "Fuck off!" to us, so we scuttled away as fast as we could and ran towards the sea where we threw down our towels and sat there panting.

"Did you see that?" asked Morgan beaming as though he'd caught someone out. "They were having sex in the bushes."

I chose not to answer but sat staring out to sea, hoping that Peter wouldn't come traipsing down to the water's edge and say something to me. I also had the feeling, by the way Morgan spoke, that he quite enjoyed seeing what was going on there and perhaps it might even have been some kind of turn-on for him. As for me, it initially was a turn-on until I realised it was Peter.

"Do you think this often happens here?" enquired Morgan, still grinning and obviously having enjoyed his voyeuristic moment.

"I wouldn't know," I replied rather coldly, not intimating that Peter and I had already experienced it. I knew that having denied knowledge of what happened in the bushes made me a liar, but I couldn't bear to explain to Morgan what had happened to me in the past.

I didn't want to turn around and look back up the dunes in case Peter might be standing on the top looking for us.

"Hey that was cool," continued Morgan, obviously still enjoying the picture he had in his mind of the event.

I was getting a little frustrated by his comments and the way he seemed to have enjoyed watching.

"Have you never seen two people kissing?" I asked rather abruptly.

"Hey they were doing more than just kissing. Didn't you see?"

Of course I knew what they were doing, but I chose not to respond to his question.

"Why are you so offish, Raj?" asked Morgan.

I couldn't tell him it was Peter I'd seen, nor could I tell him how it had upset me. Peter had been a relatively private part of my life and I didn't want to bring him into Morgan and my space that we were now trying to enjoy together. Instead, I chose to change the topic.

"Are you coming for a swim?" I asked, peeling off my shirt and wrapping my towel around me as I slipped off my shorts and pulled on my swimming shorts.

"Sure, let's go," he replied, disrobing and folding his clothes to make a little pillow on his towel.

We ran into the cool water and dived under the first wave that arrived, surfacing a few metres further out to sea.

"Wow! It's lovely and cool, isn't it?" I shouted to Morgan who was jumping and diving in the water like a dolphin.

As we frolicked in the sea, he shouted, "Raj, there go those guys from the bushes," pointing in the direction of the sand dunes.

I turned to see Peter and his friend hurriedly heading back towards the Snake Park area, but not noticeably looking in our direction. I was glad that they were going, but also saddened because I hadn't spoken to Peter for some time and I thought it would have been nice to say hello to him. I watched as they disappeared into the distance, wondering whether he would call me and try to explain his actions.

I felt a little more relaxed knowing that Peter had now left the area and it meant that I could focus my attention on Morgan.

We spent quite some time catching waves until I was exhausted from swimming and went back to our towels. I lay down and watched him still cavorting in the sea, enjoying himself. Soon he also returned to his towel and collapsed exhausted onto it.

"Swimming can be tiring," he gasped as he landed on his towel.

"But the water was refreshing, especially in this heat."

Morgan had brought a two litre bottle of cold drink which he opened and offered to me.

"Have some, Raj."

I took the bottle and held it up to my lips. The cold liquid seemed to float down my throat and instantly refreshed me. I handed it back to Morgan when I had drunk enough.

"Thanks Morgan, that was delicious."

He took a swig and then put the bottle cap back on and lay down to soak up the sun.

For about fifteen minutes, neither of us spoke much, but enjoyed the warmth of the sun and the sounds of the waves. I didn't know what was going through Morgan's mind, but Peter had briefly entered my thoughts and then disappeared.

"Raj," said Morgan, "I want to tell you something."

"What," I murmured back, without opening my eyes or looking at him.

"Remember what we had discussed after our trip to Pietermaritzburg?"

"What?"

"About being yourself and all that?"

"Oh yes. What about it?"

"I want you to know…"

I lay waiting to hear the conclusion of his sentence, but it never came. I opened my eyes and turned my head to face him, only to find that he was sitting up looking at me.

"What did you want me to know?"

He hesitated, and then lay back down on his towel.

"It doesn't matter," he sighed.

I sat up and looked at him, his chiselled chest rising and falling gently as he breathed.

"Come on Morgan, you can say it whatever it is. There's only you and me on this wide beach. I don't think anyone else is listening."

"Raj, I said that I needed time to sort myself out, well I think I have." He hesitated as if trying to decide what to say. "You know that I told you that I preferred boys. Well I've made up my mind to be myself. No one is going to force me into something that I don't want, especially if it's going to bring unhappiness to the other person."

"So, what are you trying to tell me?"

"You're really making this difficult for me, aren't you?"

"Life is difficult Morgan, and there will be far more difficult issues to face than telling me that you're gay," I replied with a slight smile on my face.

"You see… I've realised that… What did you say?"

"Have you only just realised?"

I burst out laughing and leaned across and took Morgan by the hand.

"If what you've told me is a secret, then your secret is safe with me, but I'm very proud that you have finally been able to think for yourself and make a decision that will help you as you get older. The fact that you've shown individuality shows a sense of maturity, but it's not going to be easy.

I think you know the things that I've been through with my family, but it's hardened me and made me able to overcome the various hurdles that will be put in front of me, and you have to do likewise."

"Raj, I appreciate your honesty and kindness, and it's not going to be a secret. If people want to know then they must deal with it, because I owe them nothing. I will still love my family in the same way that I used to, so nothing will change as far as they are concerned, and I would like to spend more time with you, if you'd like that."

I beamed from ear to ear.

"To hell with any laws that prohibit what I am about to do," I said, and leant across to Morgan and kissed him firmly on the lips.

When our lips released, I smiled and said, "Can I tell Sarisha?"

"Don't you think she'll want to kill you? I know she always had the 'hots' for me, but I don't like her in that way; but as a friend, I think you couldn't ask for a better friend and I hope she'll accept me in that light."

"I'm sure that she will. She's not muddle-headed like you or me."

From that moment onwards, I felt as though I was floating on air. Come to think of it, I think Morgan also felt that way, having got it all off his chest and out in the open. Peter and the bushes had suddenly vanished from my thoughts and I was happy to be good friends with Morgan. I knew that together we could get through any problem; me guiding him and him helping me.

We swam and laughed, we joked and talked, we opened our hearts to each other and told things that we had never mentioned to each other before. It was almost like an overflowing cornucopia as information flowed from the one to the other. Our pent-up emotions flowed freely and suddenly the sun seemed to be shining brighter than before.

"Do your parents know or haven't you told them yet?" I asked with a little trepidation.

"I've told my mother and she was a little upset at first until I explained everything to her and how I felt. I think once she understood that my love for her and my Dad would never alter, and then she changed her outlook. As for my Dad, I don't know what he'll say. I'm hoping that my mother will say something to him."

"I'm sure that you won't encounter the sort of treatment that I get from my father, so I really wouldn't worry, and if things really get out of hand, we'll both move out of our homes and move in together. How's that?"

We both laughed at my suggestion, but Morgan said that he might like that, which made me feel warm inside, knowing that he cared about me.

We spent the whole day on the beach in each other's company and even forewent lunch, until it was time to catch our buses to our different homes. We both caught the bus into the centre of town and then went our own ways. I felt so happy inside that I even chatted to some of the grannies and aunties, who were returning from their day of shopping, something I didn't often do.

Back home, I couldn't wait to run and tell Sarisha of the news. To my surprise, she took it better than I had expected.

"Do you think I'm jealous? I knew all along that he might be more interested in boys," she said, smugly.

"How could you?"

"I've told you it's a woman's intuition. Don't you know that we women are far more intuitive than you dull men? You men think a woman's place is only in the kitchen and that we know nothing, well you men are in for a surprise, especially when I get older and leave school."

I chuckled to myself trying to imagine how Sarisha was going to change the world, but no matter what I might have thought, I had to acknowledge that she was very much like my Aunty Selvie: wise.

CHAPTER 19

I never received any calls from Peter after having seen him and his friend at the beach, nor did I choose to contact him in case he felt embarrassed to speak to me, but I busied myself preparing for our end of the year exams and both Sarisha and I spent many an afternoon working together on our school work, and whenever Morgan didn't have sports practice, he would join us. We had become like the three Indian Musketeers: all for one and one for all!

I did wonder what had happened to Peter and then I thought of Aunty Selvie's explanation of the Apartheid system and the fact that Whites and non-Whites were not supposed to mix. I wondered also if Peter's parents had infiltrated his thoughts and told him it was 'bad' to mix with non-Whites and that was why he was ignoring me. Maybe he was finding out from them that he should never mix with non-Whites and that meant putting an end to our friendship. On the other hand, he might just have met a White friend whom he preferred over me.

However, my friendship with Morgan developed and although his father couldn't come to terms with his son's decision in life, he accepted the fact that he wasn't going to change his son's ideas and that he wasn't about to become a grandfather.

Aunty Selvie, on the other hand was over the moon, so to speak, that I had a made a friend in life with whom I could share experiences and whom I could turn to in times of need, other than Sarisha. I think that perhaps she was also relieved that I had befriended a young Indian man, rather than someone who might create problems for me in this Apartheid-run country.

"You always need a soul mate, Raj, and maybe Morgan might be yours. You've guided him through his trying times, just like I have tried to guide you," said Aunty Selvie, as we drank tea together one day. "You must remember that so long as you have love in your life, you'll be happy, and if you don't, then you must at least have hope, because without hope, you are dead."

I loved my Aunty Selvie, not only for her kindness, but also for her wisdom. I reckon that if she weren't a woman and she was nearer my age, I would have liked to have had a friend like her.

———————

1976 was an eventful year in my life. Not only had I reached the final year of my schooling, thank goodness, but it also meant that the following year I would be free to find myself a job or go to university to study. Because of my background, it was felt that I should go to university, after all, Indians place an enormous emphasis on education and we have always been a race of people who want to succeed, but before I got to university, I still had to get through my final year of schooling.

Morgan had matriculated with distinctions and left school and was in his first year at the University of Durban-Westville studying to become a lawyer, but Sarisha and I were still trying to pass our examinations. To us, life was just as mundane as it had been the year before and the year before that, until the month of June arrived.

Trouble had been brewing since the middle of June when Black school children were given a government order that the language Afrikaans – seen by most Blacks as the language of Apartheid oppression – must be used as the medium of instruction for the teaching in all schools.

A protest march was organized by the Blacks and it was unfortunately during this march that a young thirteen-year-old boy was killed. This sparked rioting and looting, fuelled by years of oppressive rule and frustration with the race laws of the country.

Although this action was taking place many miles from our homes, it still instilled within me a sense of fear; fear of the unknown. In order to try to contain the rioting, the police threw a cordon around the area in which the Blacks were demonstrating and dropped tear gas from helicopters. In the resulting turmoil, over one hundred people were killed and over a thousand were injured. To me, this was traumatic, as it was, I think, to most of the non-white population of the country. It didn't matter to me what colour or culture they were from; they were human beings who were trying to be individuals.

By the following month, the law about Afrikaans being used as the medium of instruction was dropped, but by then the protesters were protesting more against the many issues of Apartheid than merely the language issue. Rioting and lawlessness began to spread throughout the country, and within the Indian adult community; it brought back memories to some of how the Asians were expelled from Uganda by the infamous Idi Amin. Were we to be driven into the sea and killed, I wondered?

A feeling of unease spread throughout the land and, although on the surface life did appear to go on as normal, underneath there lurked nervousness, filled with anxiety and tension.

Sarisha and I tried to focus on our studies, but it was difficult, not knowing our future and that of the country. Sarisha and I tried to console each other and tried to do anything that would take our minds off the bloodshed and rioting. This included going to movies as often as we could with Morgan, when he wasn't attending lectures.

Aunty Selvie had tried to explain the volatile situation to me, and although I was now older, I still found it difficult to come to terms with the fact that humans couldn't get along together without trying to kill or maim each other. All I wanted was peace, not only in the land, but also in our community.

I hadn't spoken to Peter for nearly a year, but one day I found myself thinking about him. I looked for his phone number with the intention of saying 'hello' to him. I found my piece of paper with his telephone number written on it and decided to take a chance and give him a call. I dialled his number and waited as the phone sounded its monotonous ring. His mother answered.

"Hello, is Peter there, please?"

"Hello. I'm afraid not. He's away," was the reply.

"Oh, I'm sorry to hear that. When will he be back?" I asked.

"I'm sorry, but I don't know. He's in the army."

I fell silent when I heard the word 'army'. To me the word was the personification of death. Being a pacifist made it all the more bitter to hear that a so-called friend was now carrying a gun and possibly killing people in his own country. I simply replaced the phone without saying another word. I felt numb. To me Peter seemed a gentle soul and not someone who'd want to deliberately go out and kill people.

Two days later, I saw Aunty Selvie and asked her to explain to me how someone, whom I imagined being gentle and who might even be a pacifist could join the army to fight people in his own country.

"Who has done this, my darling?"

"Peter."

"Ah, I understand. Raj, you must understand that first and foremost, most young White men don't join the army; they are conscripted into it; and secondly, it's only Whites who have to do military training. In fact, many young White boys have fled the country because they do not want to be part of the Apartheid regime and others who have stayed, have been jailed rather than go and fight in the army."

"What do you mean by conscription and having to do military training? Surely you have a choice?"

"No, my boy. In this country all White males over the age of sixteen have to do military training; it is compulsory."

"But what if they're still at school?"

"As soon as they finish school, they have to go," replied my aunt.

"Do we have to do it?" I asked, with a tinge of panic in my voice.

She smiled at me.

"No, my boy, thank goodness. Neither us nor the Blacks nor Coloureds do it."

Before I had a chance to ask why, Aunty Selvie continued.

"You see the government feels that if they ask the Blacks, Indians and Coloureds to fight for this land, then they would have to give them the vote, and that they cannot afford to do."

"Why not?"

"Because then the ruling government would be out-voted due to our collective numbers," she smiled.

"Tell me about the riots that the Blacks started," I asked.

"What do you want to know about that?"

"Why did they riot like they did?"

"My, darling, let me put it to you like this, how would you like to study all your subjects at school through the medium of Urdu or French or Italian, when you speak none of those languages? It would be very difficult, not so?"

"Yes."

"Well, that is what the government was expecting the Black children to do. They expected them to learn all their subjects through the medium of Afrikaans."

"But why Afrikaans?"

"That's the language of the oppressor," answered Aunty Selvie, "And they wanted everyone to speak their language."

The idea of learning through the medium of another language, foreign to me, was daunting. It then made sense to me why those children wanted to riot against the idea. They felt angered by someone making them do something against their will, much the same way that I felt angered when my father had taunted me about liking boys.

After some time, the trouble abated and life resumed its casual pace at home and at school, but not before a number of young Black children had been shot and killed in their effort to defy the ruling government.

Although I was now in my final year at school, I often went out to parties with Sarisha and Morgan, when he wasn't studying. Sarisha had at this stage acquired herself a steady boyfriend by the name of Clive, who seemed quite a decent sort of guy and he accepted me for who I was, I think with some threats from Sarisha, but I had no one permanent; not that it worried me, but I often thought it would be nice to share my time with somebody special. Morgan and I did see each other regularly, but because I was still at school and he was at university, it made it a little awkward. However, he did say that should I also decide to go to university with him, we might be able to make more contact with each other. We often went to the beach over weekends, but we never bumped into Peter in our old spot, although we did see the man that we'd seen with Peter, there one day with someone else.

Amah and Apah were still together, except he was still drinking heavily and even though I was now much bigger in height and body weight, he still hit me on occasions while in his drunken stupor.

The conversations with my father were very limited and I found it better to say as little as possible to him, but I noticed that ever since the last time we came to blows when he had kicked and punched me until I was aching and bleeding, he never mentioned anything about me liking boys. I don't think he accepted it, but perhaps my mother had said something to him. Either way, it didn't worry me unduly as I had Morgan and Sarisha, and I knew that I could call on Aunty Selvie any time I wanted to.

————————

Wars had been fought on many fronts in history, and although they didn't impact directly on Sarisha, Morgan, our families, or me, I still felt for Peter whom I assumed would probably be fighting in some dangerous area, or at least be expected to go and fight if called upon. Any war must be a frightening experience, but to have it on our front door, so to speak, was even more daunting. Every day we read things in the newspapers or heard things on the radio about the fighting against the communists, but Aunty Selvie, being the wise woman that she was, kept telling us not to listen too intently as it was all propaganda.

"Good propaganda or bad?" I asked one day, as I watched her making a dish of Murgh Mussallam.

"No propaganda is good, my child," she replied. "Whatever we are told, it's bound to be made up of lies."

She was right. Her friend, Mr Walters told her about numbers of casualties that were currently being treated at military hospitals, yet the media remained silent on these casualties. When I heard his report, I immediately thought of Peter and wondered if he was safe. Should I phone his home, again, to find out? I thought long and hard about doing that, but then gave up the thought. I didn't want to speak to his mother, and if anything had happened to him, I might have to explain to his mother the connection between Peter and me.

I watched with interest as Aunty Selvie pounded the various spices to a paste. With a pestle and mortar, she ground the garlic, illaichi and jheera, along with the luangi, ginger, ground cinnamon and chilli. The aroma that filled the kitchen as she pummelled them was pungent and it filtered up through the air and into my nostrils. My taste bubs tingled and I longed for the completed dish, but I still had quite a wait. With a little water added, the dry ingredients soon formed a richly coloured paste.

As the ghee melted in the large saucepan along with the finely chopped onions, Aunty Sylvie continued on her understanding of the meaning of propaganda.

"We were told lies by the ruling government of the time."

"Like what?" I asked.

"Things like we were about to be invaded by Russian communists, not that they were regarded by any of the other nations in the world as being friendly, and that the Blacks were just like the communists; also not to be trusted. We were brought up to believe that the Black was inferior to everyone else, particularly to the ruling Whites and that was why the government chose to prevent them from gaining a good education."

I watched as the ingredients in the pan gelled together.

"Why can't we be like this dish," I said.

"Meaning what?"

"All the ingredients are different and each one adds something to the overall dish, just as we are all different and in the melting pot, we make up a colourful country."

"You mean like my sweetmeats."

"Yes!" I replied excitedly. "Yes, just like your sweetmeats. They are all different colours and each one contributes to the overall taste and when they are all placed together on the plate, it all looks so wonderful."

This dinner that Aunty Selvie was preparing was a special occasion for me. She had invited her closest friends for a meal and that now included both Sarisha and Morgan.

Michael and Vanesh as well as Sanjeev, Krish, Brian and Mr Walters were all there, as well as Uncle Harry. The food smelt delicious and I knew that the company was interesting.

When they all arrived, Michael and Vanesh again hugged Sarisha and me, as was their usual tradition, but when they saw Morgan there, Michael walked up to him, shook his hand and said, "You make sure that you take care of Raj or you'll have us to deal with", then hugged Morgan.

Poor Morgan wasn't sure how to take Michael's threats, but we all laughed and that seemed to make him feel more at ease.

"You don't have to worry about a thing, I promise that when Raj leaves school, I'll be there to take care of him, if he wants me to," replied Morgan, smiling at me.

"I'd be very careful of what promises you make, Morgan, because not only will you have to contend with Michael, but you'll also have to contend with me," said Aunty Selvie, "and I'm sure you're well aware of my reputation."

The whole group, except for Morgan, roared with laughter.

The men gathered in the lounge where Uncle Harry poured drinks for them, while Sarisha, Morgan and I helped Aunty Selvie with the dinner preparations in the kitchen.

"Sarisha, Raj tells me that you've got yourself a nice little boyfriend, is that true?" asked Aunty Selvie.

"Yes, I love him very much."

"And what does he do?"

"He's an accountant."

"Oh Uncle Harry will like him then, they'll be able to talk money whenever they meet."

The dinner was ready and so was the dessert, which Aunty Selvie and I had organised secretly without the others, knowing. The steaming pots of rice and golden curry were brought into the dining room where everyone gathered. The lids were lifted and the aromatic smells pervaded the whole room. Everyone "Oohed" and "Aahed" when they caught a waft of curry aroma. Soon people were hungrily tucking in to the food and the conversation seemed to have come to a halt.

"What are you planning for the future, Raj? Indians are by nature very concerned about their children's futures and always place an enormous emphasis on education, so I presume that you will want to go to university after leaving school," suggested Aunty Selvie.

"I thought of becoming a teacher," I replied.

She didn't seem surprised by my answer, but did comment that she thought my father wanted me to become an accountant.

"Why is it that Indians always want to become accountants?" I asked her.

"They don't all want to become accountants, but maybe it's because money is important in our lives," she replied. "You must also understand that we expect better things from you young people. Our forefathers never had much so we place so much importance on your education."

"But there's nothing wrong in being a teacher, is there?" I asked, seeking affirmation.

"Nothing whatsoever. It's an honourable profession and one that I think you could do well in, provided you put your mind to it. I'm sure that Vanesh can vouch for that?"

"I love teaching Raj," replied Vanesh, "but you must appreciate that my subject is very practical and therefore it allows for a more relaxed environment, something that doesn't happen with all subjects."

"You haven't thought of anything like becoming a doctor or a lawyer?" Aunty Selvie volunteered.

I looked horrified at her suggestion, and then smiled sweetly at her.

"You're joking about the doctor aren't you?" I replied.

"Not at all. I think you have the ability to become a good one and you have such a caring nature about you that I think you'd be successful at being a doctor."

I wasn't about to discuss this matter any further with Aunty Selvie, as I had no intentions of cutting people up or working with blood, nor did I have the intellectual ability to cope with studying to become a doctor, so I abruptly changed the subject.

"And as for being the lawyer, I think we'll leave that to Morgan, he can look after all our legal problems."

"How are your studies going at the moment, Morgan?" enquired Aunty Selvie.

"They're going well, thanks."

"Do you two get to see each other that much?" asked Michael.

"I speak to Morgan most days either by phone or if I can get to see him, but because of him studying and me still at school, it's become difficult to spend prolonged time together," I replied.

"Why don't you two take a holiday together when it's school and university holidays? You know during July or December?"

I liked the idea and grinned at Michael when he suggested it.

"Are you trying to play permanent match-maker?" I quipped.

"I don't think I have to. I think you two are most suited to each other and Morgan's a very nice young man with his head screwed on properly, and that is what you need."

"I'm sure that we'll think about it, Michael."

"I think it's a wonderful idea," concurred Aunty Selvie.

"Vanesh and I have a holiday cottage down the south coast and we often go there for weekends, so if you'd like to have a holiday together, you're most welcome to use our cottage whenever you'd like," said Michael, magnanimously.

I was dumbstruck at first and then I started to laugh.

"You're joking of course, aren't you?"

"No Raj, we're not. Both Vanesh and I like you very much and now that we've met Morgan, I think he'd be very good for you, so we'd love to spend time with you guys and let you use our home."

"I'd like to say a very sincere thank you to both you and Vanesh, Michael. I can see that Raj is a little dumbstruck at the moment, so I'd like to take up your offer and maybe we can all go there together," responded Morgan.

"This is what I want to see," said Aunty Selvie. "You boys getting together and bonding as a group; supporting one another in your times of needs and standing up for one another because, Morgan and Raj, you know that your journey from now on is not going to be smooth sailing.

The only difference is that unlike Michael and Vanesh's journey, which travelled through Apartheid rules and cultural rules, yours is embedded only in cultural ones. There are going to be times when you will have to 'suffer the slings and arrows' as Shakespeare put it, to defend your relationships whether together or with someone else, but at all times remember to maintain your dignity and your individuality. Remember who you are and be proud of yourselves; love yourselves. There will be times when there will be laughter and times when you'll cry, but if you have someone special in your life, you will always overcome you problems. And remember one very important lesson," said Aunty Selvie, "There are two things in life that we cannot do: We cannot predict when we are going to be born and we cannot predict when we are going to die, but everything in between, we can influence and control, so between the beginning and the end, enjoy life."

"Here's to life," said Michael raising his glass in a toast.

"To life," echoed the group, raising their glasses.

"Now my darling, go and get our dessert from the kitchen. Morgan I think you'll have to help carry one of the plates, so run along," ordered Aunty Selvie.

Morgan and I left the dining room and entered the kitchen.

"Raj, I like you friends and you family and I would be happy to share my life with you, so when you leave school, we'll have to talk about moving in together."

"Thanks Morgan, that's the nicest thing I've heard all night. I'd be very happy to spend my life with you, but before we can do that, we've got to get the dessert back to the dining room before people start getting worried by our absence."

The two young men walked into the dining room, beaming from ear to ear and each carrying a plate of brightly coloured objects.

"Sweetmeats are served!" I said, majestically placing my plate on the table.

EPILOGUE

The steamy heat and the white, burning sand raised my body temperature as I stood on the beach looking out over the blue sea. It was a typical summer's day where there was not a cloud in the sky, or in my opinion, a cloud in my life. It was the early 1990s and memories flashed through my head as I thought of my past and all the people who had played a part in my being here today; a young but more mature man. I was in a dream-like state feeling only the perspiration trickling sensuously down my face and chest. In the distance, I heard the gentle rushing sound as the small waves broke gently on the sea shore and moved up the beach over the coarse sand that lay right at the water's edge.

"Hello handsome," said a voice behind me. "Looking for something?"

I slowly came out of my dream-like state and turned to see where the voice was coming from. I smiled broadly and put out my arms to embrace the person who had been standing behind me.

"Hi, good looking," I replied. "I was waiting for you."

My lips met his in a gentle kiss and our arms encircled the other. We stood like this for some time and then our lips parted.

"Didn't you hear me come up behind you?"

"No," I laughed. "My mind was miles away," I replied.

"I hope your thoughts were on me?"

"I'm so glad I've got you in my life," I whispered before our lips met again.

We kissed and our bodies pressed hard together, then again our lips parted.

"I'm yours forever!" came the reply.

With our arms around each other, we walked slowly along the water's edge, oblivious of other people who might be looking at us – me and my tall, slim lover, Morgan.

ABOUT THE AUTHOR

LEW BULL has now had 11 books published by Nazca Plains. This novel adds to his collection of novels titled, *Power Buddies*; *Wet, Wild & Willing*; *The Bonds of Friendship*; *Caribbean Cruising*; *Memoirs of a Hustler*; *Shadows* and *Rough Cut*. Added to these are his two anthologies, one of exotic cocktail recipes accompanied by equally erotic stories entitled, *Cocktales* and the other, *Mystique*. His novel *Wet, Wild & Willing* was nominated for the 2008 National Leather Association (International)  writing award. Other recent anthologies that contain his work include, *Cruise Lines*; *Taken By Force*; *Boys Will Be Boys*; *Don't Ask, Don't Tie Me Up - Military BDSM Fantasies*; *Service with a Smile*; *Pretty Boys & Roughnecks*; *Special Forces and Sex Time-Travel*. He is involved in education and lives in Johannesburg, South Africa where he enjoys spending time with his partner of thirty-four years and traveling as often as he can.

tales

by

Lew Bull

MEMOIRS OF A
HUSTLER

A NOVEL BY
LEW BULL

Caribbean
Cruising

a novel by
Lew Bull

The Bonds of
Friendship

a novel by
Lew Bull

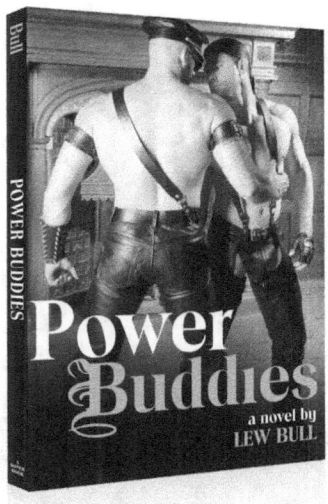

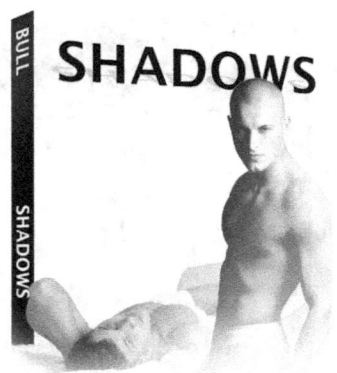

SHADOWS

A NOVEL BY
LEW BULL

THE SLAVE OF
APOLLO

LEW BULL

www.ingramcontent.com/pod-product-compliance
Lightning Source LLC
Chambersburg PA
CBHW051125260626
47170CB00005B/1675